THE GHOST IN MY HOTEL

BONNIE ELIZABETH

My Big Fat Orange Cat Publishing

The Ghost in My Hotel
My Big Fat Orange Cat
Mystery 2022

Copyright 2022
Bonnie Elizabeth Koenig

Cover image Copyright © "almoond", "yadviga", "seamartini", "alfadanz.stock" | Deposit Photo

Cover Design Copyright © Bonnie Koenig

My Big Fat Orange Cat Publishing
MyBigFatOrangeCat.com

ISBN 978-1-953363-16-9 trade paperback
ISBN 978-1-953363-17-6 large print

Chapter One

I suppose having grown the gross proceeds of the Neary-Ten Inn and Resort by well over a hundredfold in my fifteen years there, I could say I'd been successful. The fact that I lived alone in a tiny apartment at the resort with only my two cats and a best friend who was a ghost might suggest otherwise.

When you hit your late fifties and start thinking about retirement, you start thinking about what you've left behind. That was on my mind that winter as I sat in the manager's office going through the reservations. We'd had a few cancellations and a few people requesting to come in sooner due to one of those major snow storms that headed our way a couple of times a year. This one looked like a big one, probably one for the record book if the forecasts were even close.

It wouldn't be perfect for skiers, mind. They were saying plenty of freezing rain because our weather had been gorgeous up until last night. I'd even had the window open in my apartment yesterday, though the thermometer was starting to drop and now the cats were cuddling together on the afghan I kept draped over the arm and one cushion of the loveseat in my apartment.

In most places, there'd be more cancellations. We actually had *more* people who wanted to get here earlier than expected, though some were going to have to stay in Banner Elk and hope they could make it through. We were pretty well booked.

The Neary-Ten Inn and Resort had sat nestled in the mountains near the North Carolina and Tennessee border for over a century. The main part of the building, which included a huge daylight basement, a sub-basement where the help stayed, and two floors, had once been a place for the rich—though not quite as rich as the Vanderbilts and their ilk—to get away from the heat of the summer.

Now it contained the sub-basement, the basement and nine floors above plus an extra wing on one end. The old entertainment building had been turned into a restaurant that was now part of the sprawling complex.

The name, of course, came from the location and had once just been called The Inn Near Tennessee. The current owners had capitalized on that, calling it Neary-Ten Inn and Resort.

The owners had overbuilt, of course. When I had come in and taken over as manager, we rarely got rooms more than half-filled. We were just a tad bit further from the ski resorts than Banner Elk. As North Carolina wasn't known for skiing, it wasn't as if there was a huge need for more hotels for the winter.

Instead, as I noted the excitement with which people greeted a sighting of Alfred B. Calloway-Smithers' ghost in the restaurant, I began to formulate an idea. ABC Smithers as I liked to think of him, wasn't our only ghost.

Clara had once been a maid and her ghost had a habit of running down the hallway of the basement, looking behind her, tears dripping. An old man named Angus wandered around outside and would press his face to the glass windows of the main doors during the coldest temperatures. According to records, he'd gotten lost in a storm and tried to make it to the resort. He'd been found only a few feet away from what is now the parking lot, dead of hypothermia.

I had no idea what happened to Clara and wasn't certain I wanted to know. ABC Smithers had died in a duel over a woman. He was an idiot from everything I'd read.

And then there was Olive. She'd been the manager here before I started. In fact, her death had left an opening for me as the assistant manager had retired not long after, unable to deal with seeing his boss after her death. He probably hadn't appreciated her advice. Olive can be a bit bossy.

Of the ghosts, only Olive talked. And while I liked to think she talked mostly to me Olive would talk to anyone who would listen. I think I was the only one who asked questions about what it was like to be a ghost so she talked to me more often, or so it seemed to me. More than likely, she wanted to tell me how to do my job, which had been her job for more years than I'd been at the Inn.

The first time we'd chatted away, I hadn't realized I was talking to a ghost. The spirits here didn't look all see through and glowing like they do in the movies. They looked like ordinary people. I often felt a chill when they were around, but other than that, they could be normal humans dressed rather oddly.

I mean ABC Smithers had died around 1900, so his suit was hopelessly outdated. Clara wore a long white nightshirt of the sort that would have fit well in a period piece like *Downtown Abbey*. Angus wore a workman's jacket and hat that looked dated but not quite as dated as

Smithers. So far as I understood, he'd gotten lost in the forties.

Olive wore a pair of dark slacks with a brilliant peach twinset and a necklace of fake pearls. I only knew they were fake because Olive told me so.

I'd worried, coming on, that people wouldn't like a hotel with ghosts. Quite to the contrary, the guests who did see the ghosts seemed thrilled. I started building that up in our advertising. I even comped rooms for a few of the more well-known ghost hunters who inquired. Word got out.

The Neary-Ten was haunted. People came for the ghosts. They were plied with good food from our main restaurant, enjoyed the renovated spa, swam in the pool that sat in a huge windowed room that could be opened to the air during the warmest parts of summer, and enjoyed the fact that they were very nearly stuck in the middle of nowhere.

We had conventions of ghost hunters at least twice. We had a convention of funeral directors once. Apparently, they weren't immune from wanting to see what happened after. Olive had enjoyed schmoozing with them because none of them were astute enough to catch on that she was dead.

I had plenty of writers, particularly those who wrote anything related to the paranormal, come and stay here for retreats. The people who were hoping to get in before the storm came in, were, in fact, a group of writers having a cozy mystery writers conference.

I wondered how ghosts and cozies worked together. I was more of a reader of women's fiction, romance, and sometimes thrillers. The cats loved it when I found a nice thrilling tome that would keep me on the loveseat for an hour or more, sipping tea on my day off. They had my lap and the afghan which I pulled over my legs. Latte was a seal point Siamese and he'd usually capture my lap. Chai was a chocolate point and he'd normally curl up next to me, though a paw would be up on my leg, usually touching Latte's toes as if the two of them had to hold hands.

Not that I was complaining because these people wrote things I didn't read. There's no such thing as too many guests of any sort. Anyone not making it here or not getting a room would probably be able to get lodging nearby because the ice that was mixing in with this storm wasn't going to entice too many last-minute skiers. In fact, I'd heard that there'd been a fair amount of cancellations at other hotels when I called to see about recommending some of them for a night.

I leaned back from my desk, which was original to the building. It was an unfashionably large desk with heavy drawers on both sides. When computers had come along, someone had moved it out from the wall a foot or so and placed a stand for a computer box. Cords ran across the desk. I'd gotten several of those things that are supposed to make it look less messy but they still hung down and tried to tangle up my feet.

The office wasn't large enough to move the desk to any other position. I had my chair, which was a modern office chair and there were two other small club chairs in the corner. No table for visitors though. Not enough space. In fact, I'd often considered getting rid of the club chairs but then Mark, my assistant manager, and Addy, my night manager, wouldn't have a place to sit. We'd often meet in my office, which always reminded me of how useful those chairs were no matter how cluttered they made the office seem.

I'd had the old floral print wallpaper taken down and the walls painted a nice pale cream. The dark wood bookshelves behind me had been sanded down and painted cream as well, which brightened the place up. I'd asked about having those removed as they weren't very well used, but the owners weren't interested in doing so. The desk was dark wood and the floors were a lighter caramel color, original to the building. As it was an interior room, there was no window, so I needed all the brightness I could get.

Though smoking hadn't been allowed in the office for decades and the walls had been painted since, the room still had faint traces of cigarette smoke. I suspected it was the desk, but the antique wasn't going anywhere. The owners were quite proud of it, though they visited the hotel perhaps once every three or four years for a weekend, usually when the place was busy and I had little time to go over things with them.

Otherwise, given that I'd built up their revenues, they were happy to let me do my thing and carry on. Sometimes I wondered how much longer I wanted to do this.

My door remained open. The room was too small and claustrophobic otherwise. Suzanne, my afternoon front desk worker poked her head inside. "Lyle Cook is on line one."

Lyle was one of the local park rangers. We were in an unincorporated part of the county and our land abutted federal park property. Lyle was the closest thing to a police officer we had, other than the sheriffs, none of whom I was on a first name basis with. They were usually further away. Lyle's office was only about six miles down the road and he'd handle things until the sheriffs got here.

"This is Maggie," I said into the phone, though given that he'd called the hotel and asked for me, he had to figure I'd be answering. It wasn't like Suzanne was going to put him on hold and transfer the call to someone else.

"Got any rooms for this storm? I figured maybe I

better stay up close to here just in case," Lyle said. "Roads are supposed to get bad pretty quick if the forecast is anything to go by."

"We're near booked already but if you don't mind the dorms, you can stay," I said. We had dorm rooms from back in the days when the workers lived on site. Now we just used them for bad weather so we could keep the hotel running. We had some in the basement on either side of the walk to the restaurant, which connected up to my little manager's apartment on the hotel side and the restaurant storage room on the other. We also had an attic above the restaurant where, in theory, workers could sleep.

Of course, the attic was where ABC Smithers liked to pace. While he looked normal enough, too many workers hated seeing him pacing around and no one would use that end of the dorm. So now it was used as extra storage and only the bravest of us, or perhaps the most disinterested, tended to get stuff out of it.

Smithers, of course, would probably come down to the restaurant because of the weather. The writers coming in early who happened to be there when he did would probably be thrilled. So would any ghost hunters.

"I'll be over tonight if that's okay," he asked.

"Storms not supposed to start until late tomorrow," I said.

"They're now saying midday," Lyle told me, "Although, I guess it's not supposed to be real bad early on. Still, it sounded like you'd have a full house and always good to have an extra bit of security. Everyone up on the mountain is going to be run ragged once this thing comes in."

"I'll let the workers know so those that don't want to stay can swap with those who don't mind living in for a few," I said as I rang off.

That would be another thing to juggle. Workers got

extra pay when they stayed in the dorms. We didn't always need someone to do so but when winter weather threatened to shut down the roads, we kept people on. Sometimes it was overkill but other times, it kept us up and running.

The highways through this part of the Appalachians are mostly two-lane highways that hold plenty of blind curves and sharp drops on one side or the other. Add a sheet of ice and the going gets treacherous. The road out to Neary-Ten wasn't even a highway and then we had our own road from that one. All of them curved and were sometimes barely even marked.

We plowed our own road and made sure the turn-off signs were visible. In particularly bad weather, as this was advertised to be, the state closed the road just beyond our turn off. Neary-Ten would be isolated.

I always made sure to order plenty of fuel for our plows, firewood for the big stone fireplace that sat in the main lounge, and topped off the generator for the winter. We had extra fuel for it housed in a shed back behind the restaurant. In a blizzard, we'd be stuck but fortunately, we rarely got blizzards. Ice was our issue and I made sure anyone who had to go out in it to work had gear that would minimize the chances of falling.

I shook my head, settling in, checking to make sure the food trucks had arrived at both the hotel for our café and bars as well as for the main restaurant across the parking lot. If even Lyle was concerned—he was close to my age and had an attitude of having seen it all—I figured we were going to be in for some storm.

Chapter Two

Around six, I ended up helping out at the front desk. Suzanne had gone home at four so it was just Mark and one of my part-time workers. Addy, my night shift manager, would arrive in a couple of hours. We were inundated with the people who had all wanted to come in a day early and even with the three of us, there was a line.

I was at the end terminal which meant I had a view of the main doors beyond the line of people. We had a large front window outlined in wood. Next to that there was an airlock area with three sets of glass doors that led out to the covered loading and unloading zone.

It was warm enough that I noticed one of the bellhops standing in only a sweater, leaning over her podium that served as the bellhop's station. My other bellhop must have been off helping someone. The bright lights from the hotel made it impossible to see further.

I tugged at my thick blue knit turtleneck. All the warm bodies and the fire made the desk area feel hot. When it was actually cold out, the fire was nice. Several people not waiting in line were seated in the wide green and purple chairs nearest the fire. One had even picked up one of the lap robes we kept in a basket nearby, as if they were cold, which I found impossible to understand. But everyone had different comfort levels and the people relaxing clearly weren't standing on their feet attempting to check in half a hotel's worth of guests.

Going back to my work, doing a day early check-in for one of the writers, I had to admit the lobby looked good. It didn't look like the lobby of a haunted hotel with its high ceiling and the huge stone fireplace in the center. The desk was off to the right as someone came in through the main doors. The owners had talked about putting in one of those revolving doors but hadn't gotten around to it.

A long sofa and a set of chairs sat under the front window to look outside or enjoy the fireplace from a cooler distance.

The lobby bar—no one was particularly good with names when the hotel opened, I mean even the hotel name wasn't exactly good—was located just beyond the lobby area and I heard a bit of jazzy music coming from there. Around the corner was the little onsite shop where people could purchase toiletries and various snacks. If guests kept walking down that hallway they'd come to the hotel's café, which was a more casual dining experience than the restaurant across the parking lot.

Upstairs in the mezzanine overlooking the entry, we had the rather unoriginally named Mezzanine Bar. They had a softer, more laid-back feel. A large piano sat towards the front of the Mezzanine Bar and at our busiest times we brought in a pianist. I'd planned to have our local pianist there for the writers but with the weather, I'd called and cancelled. No reason to have her come out and be stuck in the hotel when she could be stuck at home with her family instead.

I finished up with the writer and a tall man that stank like he hadn't washed in a month moved up to the desk. Frank Larsen, according to his driver's license. Not with the writers. I noted he'd asked for room 785, which was one of our suites and there were rumors of it being haunted.

The upper levels were part of the addition that had been added in the seventies, when the Inn had been over-built. So far as I knew, no one had died in that room and the older ghosts all haunted the lower levels. Even Olive didn't go up into the upper rooms often, at least not that I knew of.

"I heard that Calloway-Smithers shows up before a storm. Know what time?" Frank asked. He was tall and rather cadaverous, looking more like a ghost than many of our ghosts.

"Our ghosts don't perform on a time table," I said, shaking my head. "They show up if and when they want, however, if Smithers is going to show up, I'd say any time now." I hadn't heard of sightings earlier.

Which was a bit unusual. Usually, ABC Smithers tended to get antsy a few days before a big storm. It was less than that now and he'd not been prancing around down in the restaurant. The employees over there always told me so I could log it on our social media that we'd had another sighting.

"You'd think you'd have studied his habits, given how you promote this place as haunted," Frank said. He wasn't smiling.

"We're not Disney World," I replied, keeping my face neutral as I scanned his card. Given that he was clearly interested in the ghosts and that he'd arranged his visit several months out so he could get a particular suite, I figured even if I weren't completely pleasant, he wasn't going to leave. He'd give us good ratings if he saw a ghost and realized it. Bad ones if he didn't.

Frank said nothing. His card went through. I got a license plate and information from him. Then I explained where to catch the elevators—just around the corner behind me—and what he needed to know about the wifi.

He signed the necessary paperwork and headed off to the elevator without returning to his car. I hoped that he'd parked in the lot and wasn't going to make people wait to get under the drop off area. We were busy.

"It's busy here," a heavy-set woman said. She was rolling a suitcase. "I couldn't get a spot under the drop off so I just parked in the lot. I hope that's okay?"

"That's fine. I'll be getting your plate number and make and model so we know that the car belongs to a guest," I said.

In the cities, hotels could be much stricter about parking than here. Still, we kept an eye on which cars belonged to guests so that one didn't get left here for days on end. It happened every now and then and we had to have the car towed. Once it had been a mistake on the part of an employee, for which I felt badly, but we'd asked several times if anyone had left their car in the lot and no one had volunteered having done so.

"I'm so excited to be here. I write paranormal cozies and this place seems perfect. It looks so nice, though. I was expecting something more like the old hotel in the Shining, you know?"

I looked up and smiled at her. Belinda Cassidy. I hadn't heard of her but perhaps she wrote under a pen name. Of course, I couldn't say that I read paranormal cozies—whatever that was—but I did keep track of many authors. I'd been disappointed to see no one I'd heard of on the guest register, though.

Belinda would be hard to miss. She was probably all of five foot and nearly as wide. Her blonde hair was styled nicely and she had a beautiful smile. Her outfit, a heavy sweater that came down to her knees under which she had on black leggings and adorable black boots that wouldn't do anything for her in the snow, was cute.

"I am so glad I reserved an extra night here. I tend to get so excited that I can't focus and end up talking everyone's ears off when I travel. I figured I'd give the writers a break and work it out the day before. And look at me. I don't have to worry about getting up here tomorrow."

"We have a number of people coming in early," I said. "We weren't able to accommodate everyone, but quite a number. Those we couldn't fit in will be coming up the mountain today but staying down in Banner Elk. I expect we'll be holding luggage for folks tomorrow morning before the storm gets here."

Belinda nodded.

"My friend is staying down there. She asked if she could stay in my room but I had a single king so there really wasn't a place for her to stay. Besides, she'd probably go nuts listening to me babble on."

I could appreciate the problem. I was already about to go nuts trying to listen closely enough to make appropriate responses and still continue working as fast as I could. The doors opened and a group of five women all came in together laughing and talking.

Belinda turned and waved at the group, so they must be more writers. The line wasn't getting any shorter. In fact, it was getting longer.

"Belinda!" one of the women called.

Belinda smiled. "I'm talking her ear off, so you'll have to wait!"

"No worry. Just glad to be here. We're all going to

camp out with Elsa so we don't have to drive over tomorrow. If you get everything set here, can you head over to the restaurant and maybe get us a table for eight or so?" the same woman said.

"Gotcha!" Belinda shouted back.

I hadn't thought about the people who might be doubling up if they hadn't been able to get into the hotel for the night. I made a mental note to call over to the restaurant and warn them they'd be swamped. Belinda signed her paperwork and I held up a finger for the next person while I hurried in the back to do just that before I forgot. Doing it now would give some of the servers time to get set for the evening.

A quick phone call and I was back at the counter. The next woman wasn't very happy with me for leaving.

"I would think that customers in front of you would be more important than any phone call." Her red hair was obviously colored to make her look younger than the lines on her face suggested she was. She reminded me a bit of Endora on the old television show, *Bewitched*, though her face was fuller and her hair cut in a more modern style.

"Just calling over to be sure we have plenty of servers at the restaurant. More people are here than expected," I said.

"You'd think that an organized hotel would know how many customers to expect," the woman said.

I got her card without saying another word. Some people clearly want to be angry and rude and this woman was one of them. Maybelle Sherwood. I wouldn't forget her.

The first time I ran the card, it didn't go through. I frowned, trying again. Once again the card was declined.

"I'm sorry," I said looking up at her. "But your card was declined."

"It happens," Maybelle said. "Their processing is probably too busy. Just put in anyway."

"I can't do that," I said.

"Then get me the manager." Maybelle looked down at me.

I held her gaze before very pointedly looking down at my name-tag that noted I was the manager. Mark glanced over, but said nothing. I noted the frown lines between his eyebrows though the corners of his mouth remained neutral.

"I am the manager," I said.

Maybelle sniffed. "I'm surprised you have any guests at all the way you treat us."

"Our policy states that we need an approved credit card," I repeated. "Your card was declined."

Maybelle didn't break my gaze. However, her hand darted out like a snake and grabbed the card and put it away in her wallet. She pulled out another one. This one went through.

She sniffed. "I told you it was just busy servers or phones."

"We always try twice," I said. "It was declined both times, though neither of them gave me a number to call."

Maybelle's eyes narrowed at me. I was not making a friend here at all. I had no doubt she was the sort to give me a horrible review.

"Do you know who I am?" Maybelle asked.

"I know your name from the credit card, but that's all," I said.

I did not have to wait long for her to sniff and let me know that her cozy mysteries were best sellers.

"I told them we needed to go on a retreat someplace warm. Maybe a cruise, but no. People wanted to come here, claiming a cruise would keep them from writing much," Maybelle snapped. "As if. A good writer can write anywhere, you know."

"I don't write," I said. In fact, I didn't think I had a creative bone in my body. Or maybe just one in my pinkie where I turned out crocheted afghans and scarves while watching television with the cats. I'd tried to make a sweater vest once and the results assured me that I needed to stick with simpler items.

Maybelle had to hunt around for her rental car information to get me the license plate on her vehicle. At least while she did that, she was quiet. I noticed that her clothing was lighter than most. Even her coat was only a heavy sweater. She was definitely not dressed for the mountains in a storm. If she hadn't been so annoying, I might have warned her about the chill.

Once everything was done, I breathed out a sigh of relief as I bent over to put the papers away, hoping that the next customer wouldn't notice how relieved I was to be done with Maybelle. Then, I wondered if that person knew her. After all, Maybelle was one of the writers, though the group that had hailed Belinda certainly hadn't gone out of their way to greet her.

Chapter Three

By the time we got through the check-in rush, my stomach was growling, my feet hurt, and I had the beginnings of a headache. Neary-Ten was not the kind of place that often got so many people in all at once. Now and then a group would rent a bus, but we were typically warned about that so I could have extra people on the desk. Then Mark or Addy and I could run interference with any problems and keep the line moving.

"That was some end to the day," Mark said quietly.

I nodded, feeling heavy all over. The music from the bar was louder now and I heard plenty of laughter. There were voices from the down by the café as well, so not everyone had gone over to the restaurant, or if they had, they'd found a wait. I'd noted that Belinda had come down not long after I had finished with Maybelle and headed out to the parking lot to go over to the restaurant.

The basement connection between the two buildings wasn't for the customers. Instead, outside the main building we had a covered walkway between the two. It had been put in in modern times so there was even a heater beneath the cement to keep it from getting ice covered, at least most of the time. If we ever had a real blizzard, the outdoor walk probably wouldn't be safe. In that case, I'd make signs directing people to the basement connection.

I'd seen a couple of people return looking disappointed later that evening but not nearly as many as I'd feared.

"I wonder if Smithers showed up yet," I said. He could have been wandering around in the wee hours of the morning before anyone was up to notice him. That would disappoint everyone if he did that. However, if the weather was bad, you never knew exactly when he'd show up. He was also much more likely to wander the actual restaurant rather than the attic space shortly before a storm. I had hopes that both the strange ghost hunter in room 785 and some of the cozy writers would see him.

In fact, if the storm ended up being as bad as forecast, maybe the ghost hunter would see Angus peering in one of the windows. I could hope.

"Dori told me she glimpsed him just standing and looking out when she was getting things set for lunch opening yesterday," Mark said.

I nodded, trying not to show my annoyance. Dori knew I posted about ghost sightings. She should have let me know, but the fact that there'd been a sighting of him made me more at ease with the preparations we'd made. If Smithers had actually shown up, we were going to get the storm predicted. I had no idea why I trusted Smithers showing up when he did more than I trusted scientists, but I'd learned in my time here that he had certain habits.

"Hopefully, the writers and the man in room 785 will get to see him."

Mark shrugged. "I'm heading out. I'll be back with a bag in the morning. They've moved up the storm so Addy and I swapped who would be staying. If the storm holds off a bit longer than expected and she gets in tomorrow, I'll take off for home. If I can't get out, well, we'll both stay."

"Thanks to both of you for working it out," I said. The door to the outside opened and the breeze sent the smell of wood smoke and wings over to me. My stomach growled louder.

"I think you need to get some dinner," Mark said.

I smiled. One of my regulars was there at the counter. He could handle things. If there was a big problem, he could always call or have me paged on the internal system if cell phones were out, which happened less than it used to now that we had a cell tower close by. We really were very isolated.

I had some chicken tortilla soup from the restaurant and fresh sourdough bread from the grocery store in town waiting down in my apartment, but the smell of wings had gotten me. I headed over to the bar to grab something to eat.

Like many hotel bars, this one was swathed in shadows, the black walls and floor making the place dark. The floor, of course, was shiny, and the ceiling, while mostly black, had strategically placed glass to reflect the small lights. A pony wall separated the main part of the bar from the rest of the lobby area but a couple of people had taken their drinks over by the fire. The waiters from the bar didn't take orders out there though when things slowed, they'd make a pass to pick up any empty glasses and napkins. I didn't see anything to pick up, not yet, but later, there would be plenty of cleaning to do, particularly if the hotel was essentially overfilled with people.

We'd already gotten requests for extra blankets and towels. I hoped that most of these people were only sharing for a single night.

I walked into the bar area and up to the large counter, behind which sat a variety of bottles of liquor. Instead of an ordinary mirror ours had black glass reflecting everything and making the room feel darker. The stools were covered in black vinyl as were the chairs at the round tables. Even the tables were as black as was the main part of the bar itself.

"What's up?" Teri, one of my senior bartenders asked me—though by senior I meant how long she'd work for the resort and not her age. Teri was barely out of her twenties. Her short red hair was shaved on one side and cut short in a clip on the other. She had four earrings on her ear on the shaved side. She wore a black blouse, which was the standard uniform and instead of jeans, which were approved wear in the bar, she had on black slacks.

"I smelled those wings," I said. "I'd love some. And fries. I have a feeling I'm going to need the energy over the next few days."

"It's early for the crowd," Teri said, eyeing the people in the bar. "I was wondering what was up."

"We're booked. Actually, over-booked. I heard a number of people doubling up in rooms and even planning to sleep on the pull-outs we have so they could get in before tomorrow's storm. It's not supposed to hit until afternoon but I guess a lot of folks are eager." I leaned against the bar.

"They're eager because they know some of the ghosts are more restless when the weather is bad," the man sitting on the stool closest to me said. He'd obviously been listening. It wasn't Frank the ghost hunter, fortunately.

This man was large. Even sitting, he towered over me and he was wide as well. A full beard of dark black hair curled around his face and made him look even larger.

"Is that why you're here?" I asked.

He smiled. "No. I write cozy mysteries. I always get to seminars and such at least a day before. I want a full twenty-four hours to acclimate before anything goes on and there's the early bird meet and greet tomorrow night."

I nodded. "I'm surprised more people didn't cancel, considering the weather. Quite a few people were from far away."

The man nodded. "I'm actually from Seattle. But I write cozies. And here I am about to be snowed in. What better atmosphere for a cozy mystery than to be snowed in at some hotel? It should be inspirational for writing."

I smiled a little not certain what he meant. Teri had slipped away to put my order into the kitchen. I breathed out and turned around to survey the lobby and the bar. It was early for this many people to be there. I wondered what the restaurant was like.

Just then I heard a scream, loud enough to make me jump. The big man next to me slipped off his stool, looking around as was the rest of the crowd. Even Teri came out to see what it was.

I walked to the pony wall and made eye-contact with Addy who stood at the desk, still in her jacket having just barely arrived, next to the desk worker, but she shook her head, not having a clue where the scream came from. One of the bellhops who was manning the front door was looking around, also trying to find where the sound came from.

Out of the corner of my eye I noticed a woman in a twinset set. Olive.

"What is it?" I asked.

"Basement," she said. "A red-haired woman was down by the main conference rooms. I expect she saw Clara, though I didn't feel her materialize."

I nodded.

Olive drifted away, her walk far too even for a human, though she looked solid enough. She didn't appear to notice anyone else in the bar.

I glanced over at the big man. He was frowning and then shook his head. He probably wouldn't believe it if I told him Olive was a ghost.

Chapter Four

If Olive thought someone saw Clara, then I assumed that the person was okay. Still, it wouldn't hurt to head down to the basement. I made a motion to Teri so she knew I had to leave but that I'd be right back. Chances were, another staff member had been down there and was helping the person who had screamed.

I went around to the far side of the desk, into an employee-only area where we had a staff elevator. I took that down a level. We had a daylight basement but it was still a basement and the employee elevator opened onto a hallway that was lit only by the overhead lights. The dark blue carpeting looked almost black. Once again, I made a note to consider changing out the color scheme to something paler.

Once I got to the main hallway, it was brighter, with lights on the walls as well the overheads. If we didn't have a conference or a seminar going, the doors to the main room that looked out over the ravine, or valley as the natives of this area called it, would be open. It made the basement feel less basement-y. Because we had the cozy mystery writer's meet and greet the next day, the doors that looked out over the valley were closed.

Three women sat in the circle of chairs down there all laughing.

"Did you hear the scream?" I asked.

They all nodded and giggled.

"Maybelle came running out of the hallway like the devil himself was after her. About time, I say." The woman who spoke had graying hair clipped short.

The others laughed.

"I think she rode up the elevator," another said. Also graying but her long hair was held back in a single clip.

I nodded. "She came from this way?" I pointed. It was the opposite direction from which I came. There were a few smaller conference rooms there, for when our customers wanted break-out sessions or for when someone wanted a smaller venue in the hotel. The first ghost hunter convention had just used two of those smaller rooms, the windowless ones, because it hadn't needed more space. Now that group took up all the windowless rooms and could have reserved the main conference room but they disliked the fact that there were windows. Apparently, they thought ghosts liked the dark.

Nods from the women who went back to their conversation completely unworried about Maybelle. It was probably nothing, but I walked down the hall, fairly certain Clara had been there. While there was a slight chill in the hallway, it wasn't as cool as it normally was after she made an appearance. I must have been getting slow.

One of the lights near one of the smaller conference rooms that the writers were using as break-out rooms was burnt out. I mentally reminded myself to tell someone about it to have it fixed by morning. Nothing else seemed out of place. I tried the doors but all were locked, as they should have been.

The conference's organizer, Nell Patton had been in at noon today and had started setting up. We had podiums and the audio set up in the rooms, not to mention the tablecloths and chairs. We didn't want someone to come in first thing and find the room a mess. I nodded to myself, satisfied as I came out of the hallway just as the group of women started laughing again.

It was a quieter place to sit and talk, though I wouldn't have said the atmosphere was that good. I almost asked them why they were down there but decided it wasn't my business. Besides, my stomach chose that moment to remind me I was late for dinner. So instead of talking to them a bit more about Maybelle, I took the elevator up to the first floor to pick up my wings.

Later, I'd wonder— if I had stopped to chat, would I have learned something more about what had actually happened? But by then it was too late.

Chapter Five

The next morning came altogether too early. The evening before had been quiet, probably because the people who were most worried about the weather had arrived the afternoon before. I had a feeling we'd have a flurry of activity later this morning, shortly after check out time, but before our usual check-in time. Rooms wouldn't be turned, but we did have a room where we could keep luggage for those arriving early.

I sighed, rubbing Latte's head as he stretched out next to me. Chai had already gone into the kitchen to see if I'd somehow managed to teleport in there to feed him. I heard his wails of disappointment from the bedroom. Fortunately, the apartment wasn't near any other sleeping quarters. Even the dorm had a large shared bathroom between my home and the temporary sleeping quarters for staff. In the other direction it was just the angled hall that would take us over to the restaurant.

I got up and checked the weather, noting that the main weather sources were predicting freezing rain as early as eleven. Apparently, the storm was moving faster than expected, but when it connected up with another storm from the Atlantic, it was supposed to hover over our area for some time. The low lands had flood warnings. We had ice storm warnings and even a blizzard watch for later in the evening as the temperatures dropped further.

The cozy writers might think getting stuck in a hotel in a storm was very exciting, but I found it tiresome. We had plenty of food and I'd been out the morning before to pick up my personal staples. I had cat food delivered and the boys were fine with what they had. Heck, they could probably last until next winter on what I had stockpiled.

Yawning, I made coffee and toast and put on a pair of fleece-lined khakis and paired those with my favorite brown turtle-neck under a green and brown plaid flannel shirt. It would keep me warm with the door to the outside opening and closing all the time. If I got too warm, I could change clothes at lunch time. It was a perk of living on-site.

Making sure both cats were settled, I locked my apartment and set out down the hallway to elevator that would take me up to work. I heard a noise in the dorm, but I recalled that a few night-shifters were planning on sleeping over so they didn't have to get up early and drive in before trying to get back to sleep.

Upstairs, the café was clearly busy. I heard the sounds of silverware and conversation. The enticing aroma of bacon reached me. It used to make me pine for a rasher, but in the years of working at Neary-Ten, bacon had lost some of its appeal. Not all of it, of course. I'd still munch on a piece of very blackened bacon, but the smell of it no longer made my stomach do backflips.

Suzanne was at the desk, looking at something on the computer. A few guests were in the reception area, but no one was asking questions of her.

"How are things?" I asked.

"Quiet," Suzanne said. "I had a flurry around six but nothing I couldn't handle. And I'm yours if you need me. I moved into the dorm earlier this morning."

Check out was easier than ever with computers. Mostly people just needed to turn in their keys and maybe grab a printed receipt. Abby made the rounds after midnight, pushing printed receipts under doors, but someone always had questions, especially if they'd charged food to the bar or the restaurant. Still, check out wasn't the mad house it used to be when everyone had to go up and turn in a key and settle their bill.

"We might get some early check-ins with the storm. Let me know. It's you and me until Mark and Sydney get in around noon or so," I said.

"Addy is staying over, just in case Mark can't get in this morning," Suzanne said.

"It was just cloudy when I looked out a few minutes ago," I said. And Mark was likely to drive over early if it looked like freezing rain would begin sooner than expected.

"She was worried," Suzanne said and shrugged.

Fortunately, I had enough overtime to pay both Addy and Mark for staying over as it looked like they both would be. The owners wouldn't be terribly pleased but I'd blame it on the weather if anyone asked. It was the truth. They ought to appreciate such dedicated employees. Of course, Addy probably didn't want to be stuck in her apartment, which I'd heard had a tendency to lose power quickly. I wasn't sure what Mark's story was.

Three women in a group got out of the elevator. One of them was Belinda. She was dressed in a lovely turquoise dress that fell to her knees. Black boots came mid-calf, reaching up over leggings that had the sheen of being fleece lined. As they passed the desk to go back to the café, Belinda waved. One of the other women also held up a hand in what could have been a wave.

I waved back.

"Are those some of the writers?' Suzanne asked.

"The woman in turquoise is, so I guess the others are, too."

"The weird guy in 785 came down this morning and asked if I knew when the ghost up there normally appeared," Suzanne said.

"Did you tell him we'd never seen the supposed ghost in room 785?" I would hate to have Frank upset, but I wondered what Suzanne's take was.

"I gave him the standard answer," Suzanne said. "I really wonder why people think that room is haunted."

I did, too. I'd asked Olive multiple times when she'd appeared in the apartment but she'd never heard of the ghost in that room. As I looked back, I noticed that all the rumors about that suite had started after I'd begun promoting the hotel as being haunted.

"I think it was just someone trying to get in on the excitement of seeing a ghost and then others had a light flicker or something," I said. Given how far we were from civilization, our lights flickered often. Fortunately, we had backup generators and I had no doubt we'd be using them if this storm was even half of what was expected.

The internal phone rang. I picked it up.

"This is Maggie," I said.

"You need to come down to the Skyler room," a woman said. Probably one of the maids. I didn't recognize her voice, but I didn't deal directly with most of the cleaning crew. They had their own managers and supervisors.

"What's going on?" I asked.

"Please. Just come." The phone was hung up.

"Someone wants me down in the Skyler room," I said.

Suzanne frowned. "That's not one of the rooms the cozy writers are using, is it?"

I clicked onto the computer to double check. Skyler was next door to one of the break-out rooms but wasn't on their list. However, sometimes groups would try doors to see if they were unlocked. I'd been down there last night and all doors were locked.

"Nope," I said as I turned to leave.

The basement was busier, with early-bird writers beginning to hover around the tables that would be used for check-in, although the event didn't officially start until the evening. With the timing messed up due to the storm, many were probably feeling at loose ends and hoping to find out if anyone had planned new events. Too bad Nell Patton hadn't come up with something.

I hurried down the hall, barely noticed. No one knew me, which might be a good thing.

A young woman, barely more than a girl, really, stood outside the Skyler room in a maid's uniform. She was holding her hands together, fingers linked, bunching them together and pulling them apart. Her face was pale. I wondered if she were naturally pale or if something had frightened her. Most of the housekeeping staff that worked on this level had run into Clara. If they stayed, they could handle her.

"What is it?" I asked, getting closer.

The girl just pointed at the door. "I was vacuuming and checking doors. This one was unlocked. I pushed it open to see if I needed to clean in there and that's when I saw it. I didn't know what to do…"

She seemed about to cry.

I opened the door that she'd closed again. The room

had chairs folded up neatly against the far wall. A few tables were on their sides. It was clearly serving as a staging room for any extras that might be needed for the writers. Our main storage area was a level down and our events staff often brought up more than was needed and set it in an unused room, like this one, if there were any.

I swiveled my head, wondering what the woman saw when I noticed the dark red on the carpet. Our carpets didn't have red on them. I'd had too many laughs about hotels with red patterns in the carpet that looked like blood. Just what we needed in a haunted hotel. I stayed away from that color, and burgundy, which is why the basement had dark blue carpet with lighter blue flecks.

A chill went down my back and my heart started to pound. Something was wrong. I followed the trail of red towards the wall where I noted a shock of very orange colored hair smeared in with the darker red-brown.

I gasped out a breath even as a hand flew to my chest.

Without even thinking, I took a few steps over to the crumpled form, hoping, but knowing I was wrong, that someone was playing a joke and this was a pile of clothing with a wig. But no. It was a woman. Closer, I noted her face and the clothing.

Maybelle Sherwood.

Still wearing the outfit she'd had on the night before. Her skin was almost bluish, as if chilled. I touched her and felt the unnatural coolness of her body. She was dead. And had been for some time.

I pulled out my cell phone to call the Sheriff's Department. We'd need more than just Lyle for this.

Chapter Six

Unfortunately, though, the storm was already ravaging the mountains even without having hit. There were two huge pile ups on the roads leading up here from the west and most of the deputies on duty were out there. A couple of others had been dispatched to rescue some folks who lived in the area and had already gotten stuck. We'd be waiting.

Instead, they promised to send Lyle if he were available. Moments later, I got a call from Lyle and I was able to tell him what was going on, keeping my voice low, though I doubted the writers would hear. But I really didn't need a conference full of mystery writers knowing there was a body in the next room. For now, maybe they'd just believe Maybelle wasn't going to show up. And for those who had already seen her, maybe they'd assume she'd left.

Lyle promised to be there within the hour. He asked that I lock up the door. I did so and then called someone from hotel security to sit outside and make sure no one entered the room. Those tasks done, I sent the maid, on her way.

"Are you working all day today and staying in the dorms?" I asked.

"I don't live far," she said. "And I have all-wheel drive. I'm sure I can get home."

I raised an eyebrow. "I'm sure someone can lend you some clothing if that doesn't work out. Talk to your supervisor and only them. If we can cover your shift, you can head home now. You've had a shock and I know the sheriff will be able to find you if they need you." And if she were home, then she couldn't talk to anyone else about what had happened. I really didn't need the staff gossiping where the guests might hear.

The maid nodded at me. "I think I'll be fine. Maybe I'll just see if I can get a few minutes to grab a hot tea or something. I feel kind of cold."

"It's better if you go home, but if you can't, don't say anything about what you found to anyone else. I don't want to spook the guests."

Perhaps a poor choice of words as the maid tried to hide a trembling smile before she turned to go.

I shivered, suddenly feeling cold. I looked around, expecting to see Clara. Instead, Olive appeared.

"I didn't see anything," she said, with something approximating a sigh.

"Hear anything?" I asked.

"I had no idea she was there, but it looks like she was probably dead for several hours. Maybe since last night."

"Those were the clothes she wore when she checked in," I said. "I remember because she was difficult. I didn't get the sense that she was well liked by her peers either."

"Clearly." Olive said, widening her eyes.

I smiled at her, getting her rather dark joke and headed away from the writers. We had a back staircase down that way and not much else. We should be able to talk without anyone listening in, except possibly for the security guard and part of their job required them to sign a form that said they wouldn't talk about what they learned at the hotel.

"I hope," Olive said when I leaned back in the corner against the wall, "that Lyle is up to this."

"He takes care of a lot of things for the police. I'm sure he'll be able to preserve the scene as well as possible. Fortunately, we weren't planning on using that room," I said.

"But this is a conference of mystery writers. Just think, he'll have to outsmart a bunch of people who plan crimes for a living!" Olive said. She sounded pleased.

I couldn't say I shared her enthusiasm. She wasn't wrong about the writers, though I doubted most of the group, which tended to be women middle-aged and older, would actually be able to carry out a murder all on their own. And if they did, I had images of poison in their tea, ala Agatha Christie.

"Do you really think one of the writers could have murdered her?" I asked, softly. The word murder felt odd in my mouth. It was possible Maybelle had fallen and hit her head on the wall, but there was no real reason for her to be in the Skyler Room. And it had been locked earlier in the evening. I'd been down there to check.

I thought about the scream I'd heard. I'd assumed it was someone who saw Clara. Even Olive had thought so. And didn't the writers down there say something about it? I tried to remember, but the last few days all bunched together in my mind.

"Who else?" Olive asked. "Unless she was secretly meeting a lover here, but she didn't exactly seem like the type, did she?"

I had to admit Olive was right. Maybelle didn't seem like the type to be meeting a lover. Her attitude was so negative. If I were meeting someone I adored, I'd have been too excited to be that difficult. Well, it wasn't my job to find out who had murdered her, if that was what had happened. It would be Lyle's.

"I suppose someone could have accidentally knocked her around," I said slowly, thinking. "And then they got scared. Maybe they hated her and didn't want anyone to think they'd purposely killed her."

Olive made a face and shrugged before fading out and then fading back in. I sighed. She definitely didn't like that particular theory and she'd probably come up with something new which she wanted to share. I didn't exactly have time to listen to her. After all, my job was to run the hotel and keep my guests safe.

"I'd think that a writer would have had a better idea than just leaving her there," Olive said.

"Have you got any?" I asked, putting a hand on my hip.

Olive gave me a long look. She fingered her fake pearls before speaking. "I'm not a writer am I? But wouldn't that be a fun thing? To write mysteries. I bet plenty of them have wonderful ideas. I ought to go and read over some shoulders!"

And like that, Olive disappeared.

I shook my head. I could have used a ghostly presence to listen in but Olive appeared more interested in her own amusement than in finding a murder.

Chapter Seven

It took Lyle nearly an hour to get to the hotel. I was at the desk with Suzanne, reprocessing a check-out when he arrived. Suzanne was checking in one of our authors who had just arrived. They'd been lucky to make it in with all the accidents.

Lyle waited while I finished.

"Skyler Room," I said. "I have security down there and they can let you in."

"I'll need to interview you when I'm done," Lyle said.

I looked around the reception area. Only a couple of people were walking across the carpet and they weren't looking at us. No cars drove into the unloading zone. I didn't even see any cars outside, although the light was as dim as it normally was in the evening. The low gray clouds were definitely taking a toll on visibility which was probably why the sheriffs were tied up with traffic accidents. It definitely appeared to be raining already.

I nodded at Suzanne who was aware of Maybelle's death and slipped out from behind the desk. She knew she could call someone if needed. Fortunately, this time of the morning wasn't normally busy and Suzanne was one of my most efficient employees. Mark had come in a few minutes ago, talking about traffic. He was upstairs getting set up in a room, one of the perks of being an assistant manager.

"What took you so long?" I asked Lyle glancing at the time as we headed downstairs. He'd come in the night before and bunked in the dorms but had gone out again before I'd been called downstairs. No doubt he'd been making rounds on the borders of the forest to be sure there weren't any foolish people attempting to camp out during the storm.

"The car pile ups that have the sheriff department tied up. Both of them are just before the turn off to Neary-Ten. Some of your authors might not be getting here. In fact, the woman your desk worker was checking in was lucky to get here at all. The accident happened early," Lyle said.

"How did you manage it?" I asked.

"I can drive on the shoulder and go around," Lyle grinned. "And the sheriff on duty knew where I was heading. I know they want to get out here. They're worried about a crime scene. Forensics is geared up and on their way, but their bus is wider than my Jeep and isn't quite as steady on the shoulder, so they might have to wait a bit longer to get through."

The highway shoulder was narrow in some places. I didn't blame the forensic crew for not wanting to drive it. I had a feeling the young woman who was checking in, younger than most of the other writers I noted, probably took the shoulder as well, unaware of how dangerous it would be if she got too close to the edge.

Mark would have come the back way. It wasn't much of a back way, the road narrow and winding and probably far more dangerous than the shoulder, but he lived in the area and knew it. And likely he'd already heard about the traffic backups which was probably why he'd come in sooner than expected.

Downstairs, the security person sat in a chair just outside the Skyler room. The doors to the main conference room were closed but there was some laughter coming from inside. Probably writers talking and planning out what to do for the day seeing they all had to arrive early if they wanted to arrive at all.

"Mystery writers?" Lyle asked reading the sign.

"Just what we need, right?" I said. "The woman in the Skyler room was with them."

Lyle pulled out a notepad and made a note. He paused before the doors. And looked around. A single woman came out of the conference room, carrying a water bottle. She headed in the opposite direction, towards the bathrooms.

"Who found her?"

I gave him the maid's name and what she was doing there. "She found the door unlocked and thought she might have to clean in there. It was locked last night when I went around and checked. All the doors were."

"Who had keys?" Lyle asked.

"All the managers, the security people, front desk staff. There's even one behind in my desk and I'm sure there are extras in the security office," I said.

"So, easy to get," Lyle said.

"If you know where to look." It wasn't like I handed out master keys to just anyone.

Lyle paused at the door and then nodded to Wayne, the security guard, a skinny young man with red hair who looked like he'd be more at home in front of a computer than doing security at a hotel. He jumped up and unlocked the door.

Lyle put on a pair of gloves and opened it, gingerly, although given that both the maid and I had already touched the knob, I doubted there were any finger prints to worry about messing up.

A stink floated out from the room with the door was open. I hadn't been as aware of it earlier, but now I stepped back. Metal and something else, something rotting. Of course, something was, though it seemed impossibly fast for a body to rot already.

I stood back while Lyle stepped into the room. Without thinking, I brought a hand up to my nose. Wayne, I noticed, nodded and turned away, also stepping a bit further back from the door.

The smell could attract attention. I stepped down the hall a bit, trying to determine if it spread very far. The room next door was still closed and I checked the knob. Still locked. I hoped the authors didn't start asking to use the break out rooms.

I didn't want them noticing the smell. Of course, when forensics got here, they'd likely notice them, although perhaps the forensic workers would be able to get in and out before too many people gathered to socialize or whatever they were doing in the large room.

While I'd built up the hotel's reputation, it was still geared mainly towards smaller conferences and seminars rather than large conventions. I didn't have any other rooms to move the writers to. Everything I had was on that floor in that part of the hotel.

It was bad enough that people could be injured or killed just trying to get here. I was glad the hotel couldn't actually be liable for that, but even so, this was not a good beginning to a conference. It made me wonder why the writer's had chosen our hotel in the middle of winter to have a conference. I knew they were mystery writers and we had plenty of mystery with our ghosts, but even so, in winter, you'd think they'd want to escape the cold and go somewhere warm.

The gray flat light that had drifted into the lobby when Lyle had arrived suggested that the weather was changing quickly. I poked at my weather app, noticing it reported that it had started to rain, which I knew. Freezing rain, which I didn't. And it was coming down hard. This deep in the basement without any windows, I had no way of checking what raining hard meant. Usually, in the south that meant a deluge, so very different from the gentle rain I'd grown up with in Oregon.

I heard a shutter click several times. Lyle was taking photos. The doors to the main conference room opened and the noise of conversations spilled out, covering the sounds he made.

A chill descended. At first, I thought it was from the air in the main room but then a woman in an old-fashioned dressing gown appeared and ran down the hallway. She looked back at me, her eyes terrified. Then, unexpectedly, as if she could see me, she winked.

Clara was creating a diversion as she passed by the main room, keeping the group of about a dozen authors from paying any attention to what was going on at my end of the hall. The women, and the group was all women, though there were several men who were part of the conference, all turned to see her. A few took a couple of steps to follow. Now, the conversations got louder. They were either certain they were being punked or that they'd just seen a real ghost. I suspected it was both at the same time given Clara's wink.

While there were those who looked back towards me, most turned to stare at where Clara had disappeared. Several women walked down the hallway away from me. A couple hugged each other, either for warmth or from fear and headed out towards the main elevators.

"That worked, didn't it," Olive said, appearing beside me.

"Shit," Wayne mumbled behind me. While he'd probably been used to Clara, he wasn't quite used to Olive, who was far more mobile and unpredictable than our other ghosts.

"Your idea?" I asked.

Olive nodded. "It's too bad Clara isn't able to remain visible further down the hall. She pushed it this time, but something stops her from going further. Perhaps she was murdered nearby?"

"She doesn't know or she won't tell you?" I asked. Olive and I had discussed the reason someone might become a ghost and why they tended to remain in a certain area. Even Olive had no idea why she was able to appear almost anywhere she wanted within the main hotel, though she had plenty of theories and we discussed all of them— or at least the ones Olive cared to share.

Clara had been a maid of some sort and from what Olive had gathered—Clara wasn't a talker—she'd cleaned many rooms but she seemed trapped in this part of the basement. For some reason Olive wasn't able to appear in the restaurant so she'd never talked to ABC Smithers. And try as she might, she hadn't come across a ghost in room 785.

"If Clara knows, she hasn't told me," Olive said. "Not all ghosts can remember everything. And the longer I'm dead, the less I seem to remember of my mortal life. There's a pull to let go, though in my case it seems very light. The hotel was always of such interest to me."

Which was probably why she'd died of a heart attack in the apartment where I lived. I hadn't known that when

I'd taken the job and I'd not been pleased to learn about it, but I'd already moved in and other than occasionally bothering my cats, Olive wasn't horrible to share space with.

She drifted down towards the writers. More were dispersing but a few were looking down towards where I was. I hoped they didn't suddenly notice Olive. When she moves, she doesn't look quite human. Her feet move as if she's walking but her figure remains even, like an image being projected, even though she looks real enough.

A couple of women rubbed their arms as they left.

Behind me, Lyle came out of the room and closed and locked the door.

I turned.

"If the coroner can't get through, is there a place to keep the body?" he whispered, mindful of the women milling around not far away.

I sighed. "All the walk-ins are full because of the storm. I wasn't sure how long it would be until we could get out."

"Any way to move things around?" Lyle asked.

I thought about our walk-ins. The one near the bar was the smallest. It would mean running around for the workers, but perhaps I could get someone to shift the food in there to other places. Unfortunately, I'd overstocked it, knowing that poor weather and a conference would make it popular. The main restaurant was also well-prepared, though not overstocked. I figured that the inclement weather would keep a fair number of people at the hotel.

"I'll see what I can do, but it won't be immediate, you know," I said.

Lyle nodded. "I can't do anything until forensics gets here. I think they're estimating another 45 minutes. They're also asking if you'll have a place to stay as they can't be certain of getting back out again."

"We have rooms. Yesterday we were overbooked but

we had a flurry of check outs earlier this morning. The hotel itself is only about three-quarters full and that's mostly thanks to the writers."

I'd bill the county for the rooms, but I didn't really expect to get paid, at least not any time soon. That's one thing about bureaucracy, it doesn't move quickly.

"Anything else?" I asked. I glanced over my shoulder. Olive had either glided into the main conference room or she'd disappeared. No one was oohing or screaming so I figured she'd entered the room and was looking around. She's surprisingly nosy. I suppose if I were a ghost with nothing better to do, I'd be nosy as well.

"I'll need to start interviewing guests, which means people will know about the murder. Any suggestions on where to start?"

"I think the dead woman came for the conference. I checked her in. Her name was Maybelle Sherwood. Those are the clothes she was wearing and it's her hair color and as far as I recall, that's her face, too," I said. Her features hadn't stood out to me, but the face on the woman looked like the Maybelle I recalled. "She's one of the writers. She didn't seem very pleasant and I noticed that groups who greeted each other didn't bother to greet her."

Lyle made notes.

"Anything else?"

"Last night as I was waiting for some dinner, someone screamed from down here, quite loudly. I even heard it up in the bar and the music was fairly loud. It surprised me. The stairs aren't that close. When I got down here to check, there were some older women who all seemed to be part of the writer's group in the little lounge at the bottom of the stairs talking. They said Maybelle came running out of here, so she'd run away from this area," I said. I frowned thinking about it.

That didn't make sense at all.

"You're sure about the direction?"

"There's only the conference rooms down there," I said. Thinking back, I wondered if I were wrong and Maybelle had run towards the rooms, but if she was being chased, as was the suggestion, it didn't seem like she'd have run into an area she didn't know. Much smarter to run to the stairs and elevators, which is the impression I had of what she did when the woman talked to me. But then, when had she entered the Skyler room and why?

There was a set of restrooms near the back stairwell, so it wasn't impossible she'd gone to explore where the conference was and used the toilet. It was unlikely she'd gone running down there if she were fleeing someone. If she'd gotten scared of Clara, Clara fled in the direction I'd been told Maybelle ran as well.

Lyle made a note. "If you find out who those women were, I'd love to talk to them first. Also, I'm going to need to see a list of all the writers."

I sighed. No one was going to be happy about this, but the hotel did have a list of the writers from the organizers. I could insist that the hotel valued our guest's privacy, but didn't particularly see the point in trying to protect a murderer, especially when a court order would force to me turn over the information anyway. Besides, Lyle would likely go to Nell and I doubted the conference guaranteed any sort of privacy.

Chapter Eight

By the time I got Lyle settled with the list I had from the conference organizer, it was just past noon and the storm had definitely arrived. The windows where the wind hit were already covered in ice making it impossible to see through the frozen swirls made by the storm. The bellhops were all inside now, looking out through the doors, which, thanks to the portico, fared better than most of the windows.

Poor Angus' ghost wouldn't be seen even if he were to appear. I shuddered to think of someone out there unable to find help, so close, yet so far away.

The smell of bacon had given way to hamburgers and fries. Once again, having worked here as long as I had, the smell of French fries no longer made my mouth water. I still ate them sometimes, though. I'm not a complete food cynic.

Soft music came from the bar to invite those around inside, though this early there were few takers. I had heard that writers tended to be heavy drinkers, but if that was true of this group, they didn't start before noon. At least not in public.

I checked over the morning's receipts. We'd had a couple of early check-ins as I'd expected, but Suzanne had noted that both had places to stash their luggage until their rooms were ready. Housekeeping had been notified to clean those rooms first.

A red flashing light alerted me to something outside. The forensic truck, or bus as they called it, had pulled up into the portico. Both bellhops were standing up straight. I saw one frowning. I sighed, hurrying over to the door. I had thought not telling anyone about the body was a good idea but now more people would have questions.

"This way," I said as the medics came in, carrying cases with them.

I led them to the back elevator, trying to avoid as many prying guest eyes as I could. Fortunately, the lobby remained quiet, though the few people hanging out were definitely curious about what was happening.

Safely inside the employee elevator, I pressed the down button.

"So where is the body? Is the area secure?" one of the forensic technicians asked. Both of them were fairly tall men, one with blonde hair and one very dark. Given their builds and the rugged handsomeness of each face, I had no doubt that there were few women who wouldn't swoon over at least one of them.

"She's in one of the conference rooms—not one being used," I hurried to add. "The door is locked and I have security outside the room to make sure no one tries to get inside."

They nodded, not asking any further questions. In the basement, I led them down the hallway. I was disappointed to see a few of the cozy writers sitting around talking. As they took in the two men following me, still dressed in parkas carrying heavy cases, both of which stated that they were from the County Sheriff, I thought I saw eyes widen and eyebrows raise.

Just what we needed. Any number of wanna-be amateur sleuths trying to solve the puzzle of who killed Maybelle Sherwood. I hoped that no one would keep things from Lyle simply because they wanted to be the hero in their own personal murder mystery.

The two men set their cases down and pulled off their heavy jackets and started gearing up to go into the room.

"Who was in there?"

"The maid who found the body. Me. And Lyle. Lyle took photos while he was in there. I touched her skin feeling for a pulse just to make sure. I'm not sure if the maid did the same," I said. "Lyle was gloved when he opened the door. The security guard had to put his hand on the knob to open the door. I'm sure I did as well along with the maid."

Which meant that there weren't likely to be useable prints on the knob.

To their credit the men just nodded.

"Was the room to be used and you closed it off?"

"It was only used to store some extra chairs and tables. I think there are more tables and chairs downstairs if we end up needing them," I said. Although with the weather, we might not. Any writers who hadn't managed to come in early weren't likely to get here.

"So only staff should have been in here before they found a body?" the one pressed again.

"Except for Maybelle and, if she didn't just fall, then whoever killed her, which might not be staff," I said. They didn't need to think that I hired murderers.

They acknowledged my comment, but said nothing.

Wayne went to unlock the door, but they stopped him and asked for the key. Suited up, they went in to do what it was forensic investigators did. Wayne went back to his chair. I left him to remain on guard duty while the men did their work.

Upstairs, Suzanne had gone off to lunch, leaving another worker at the desk. Catching up on what was happening, I heard Lyle call to me from my office.

Walking in, I saw him seated in the chair behind my desk. If I were to sit down, I'd have to sit in one of the two chairs off to the side. It felt weird that I couldn't sit behind the desk in my own office.

"I'll need someone to go find people for me to question," he said. "Do you keep photos of guests by any chance?"

I shook my head. We looked at a picture ID to be sure they were who they said they were on the credit card but didn't capture any guest images. I'd know some of the people that had checked in with me. The other desk workers might recognize others. And whether we did or not really depended upon whether that person was memorable in some way. Maybelle, unfortunately, was. And for all the wrong reasons.

Lyle sighed. "Do you have cell numbers to call them?"

"We get it on the initial intake, but it's on the computer. It's not something we use. Nor is it information we give out. In fact, we state that on the forms, so I'd need something official in order to share that information with you. I'm sorry," I said.

While it might be the right thing to do to give out the information to help Lyle, I'd always been advised by legal that we needed a warrant in writing to give out any guest's information on our system. The only reason he had the names he did was because I'd had a list of names from the conference organizer, which meant it wasn't even in our system, not really. And by giving it to him, I had just sped up the process. At least that would be my argument if anyone had an issue.

It might be splitting hairs, but I knew our attorneys would make a big deal about that if someone complained. Hopefully, if we kept our other guests safe, no one would.

Lyle frowned at me but he knew my hands were tied.

"Can someone go find some of these people for me?" he asked. "If you have access to any photos can you look and see if you recognize the women from downstairs last night?"

"I'll walk around the hotel first and see if I can find them," I said. "I'll send Mark around, too. He'll probably recognize anyone who's not down in the conference area."

"And don't go talking," Lyle said. "Bad enough that I have a bunch of mystery writers who might have noticed the forensic team coming in. Is the truck still sitting under the portico?"

"Last I looked." I hadn't actually noticed when I came up, but they'd left it there and I doubted anyone had jumped in to move it.

"I'll see you shortly," Lyle said, as if I knew exactly where I was going to find women who might have murdered one of their own.

Chapter Nine

When the four women I was searching for weren't in the any of the public places in the main building—and I'd done a tour of the main conference room, drawing a frown from one of the women at the registration table—I went through the long basement hallway to the restaurant.

Olive waited near my apartment where the hall angled away from the main building.

"Have they determined who did it?" she asked.

"Have you?" I returned, slowing my pace. Olive could slip into hotel rooms without being noticed, much.

"I've been trying to listen in but my hearing isn't very good unless I'm in a material form and then it's much harder to eaves drop and not be noticed." Olive made a face.

"Can you see?" I asked.

"Usually?" Olive knew there was something up.

"When I went downstairs yesterday after someone screamed, four gray-haired women were downstairs talking and laughing. They told me Maybelle had gone running away from where we found her body. Lyle wants to interview them first."

"Do you know how many of these women have gray hair?" Olive asked, putting a hand on her hip. She didn't quite roll her eyes but it was a near thing.

"I remember one was very slender and in jeans. She had short hair. Another had longer hair pulled back in a braid. It was definitely gray, not white," I said.

"I'll go look but I can't guarantee anything. I assume all your running around has been looking for them in the public rooms?"

"And I'm off to the restaurant," I said.

"I think I'm glad I'm retired from this job," Olive said.

I gave her a long look.

Olive just smiled rather mysteriously, as if she had a secret, and I didn't doubt she had many, and drifted towards the hotel before fading out. I hurried down the corridor. This part of the basement was underground. While it was wide enough for a large cart to be pushed through and the walls were painted a light beige, it always felt dark to me. No light quite hit all the shadows that lurked near the baseboards.

Normally, it didn't bother me, but this was the sort of place where someone would run from a killer in a horror movie. Not that I watched many of them, not any longer. There were no doors, no side corridors. You'd have to outpace your attacker for a good long time before you had any hope of finding help or a hiding place. It wasn't a good place to go walking when you knew a murderer was around.

As I walked, I almost wished I'd grabbed my coat and braved the cold. We had tarps that would shelter the walk from the worst of the wind and the freezing rain. I wouldn't have gotten too cold.

Of course, by the time I thought about that, I was closer to the restaurant than I was to my apartment. I had no desire to go back. Of course, as I reached the storage area of the restaurant, I realized I'd have to walk back through the corridor, probably alone, unless I was lucky enough to find the group of women I was searching for and made them join me. But then, I might be walking with a group of murderers which was the exact thing I was trying to avoid. I sighed. I couldn't win.

I climbed the stairs rather than using the elevator and reached the kitchen area. The kitchen was a typical industrial kitchen with plenty of stainless steel and pale tile.

"What's up?" one of the line chefs called. He was busy doing some prep for one of the meals.

"Just need to check and see if one of our guests is out there," I said.

"Intercom not working?" he asked. A couple of the other kitchen workers looked up, including the main chef on duty.

"Don't have a name," I said.

I noted the puzzled looks. Normally, if a particular guest was wanted, we'd have a name. I doubt we'd ever gone looking for someone I had only seen once without have some idea of who they were.

"Long story." I waved at them and headed out towards the main eating area.

The swinging doors let out to the big room done in dark wood and deep purple upholstery. White table cloths brightened the room band we had the deep purple, or plum as they'd been called, napkins bringing the colors together.

The windows that looked out over the parking lot were angled differently than the ones at the hotel so less ice obscured the view of what was now mostly snow falling. A light white dusting covered the tops of the cars nearest the restaurant. The bright black and white of the bus that the forensic technicians had arrived in stood out.

The room was filled to capacity. I saw Frank, the man from Suite 785, sitting in a chair by the front door. I wasn't certain if he were waiting to be seated when someone left or if he was just waiting for ABC Smithers to appear. Or not. I looked through the sea of people, noting that over two-thirds of them were women, mostly white women.

As Olive had noted, there were plenty of women here with gray hair. I saw one woman with short gray hair and for a moment I thought I had found one of the writers I was looking for, but when she looked up, I noticed the cut was all wrong and her face was much rounder. Another group of grays sat on the other side of the room but they weren't the women I sought either. I walked through the restaurant, though I wasn't going to go outside. I just wanted to be sure I hadn't missed a group.

"Checking for the ghosts?" Frank asked as I got close.

I smiled. "Just making sure everyone is comfortable. Are you waiting for a table?" I asked.

"Yes and no. I'll have something here to make sure your servers get a tip, but mostly I'm just hoping to catch Smithers. I have my equipment with me. I hope that doesn't bother him." Frank lifted a backpack up. I had no idea what sort of equipment he meant, but over the course of working in the hotel, I had seen people with square devices holding them out. Other visitors had something that looked rather like a radar detector that they pointed around. Once, we'd had another customer scream thinking it was a gun.

"Good luck," I said. I appreciated that he knew he ought to order something if he were spending time in the restaurant. For that alone, I could wish Smithers would appear for him. And maybe, just maybe, I'd find the time to ask him about the ghost in 785.

I left the restaurant to hurry back along the corridor to the main part of the hotel. I was too busy trying to think if there was any where I hadn't looked for the women to make note of the shadows and the fact that anyone after me would have a long length of hallway for me to run. Worse, if they had a gun, it wasn't exactly a place where I could weave and dodge.

Who was I kidding? At my age, I'd be lucky to jog down the corridor being chased by a mouse. There was no way I'd be weaving and dodging bullets like the characters in my favorite thrillers did.

Arriving back at the main part of the hotel, I heard people talking even before I passed my door. Perhaps I'd get lucky and the women I was looking for would be down there. They weren't, but I did notice several women crowded around Wayne.

I sighed. Word was out before we wanted it to be.

"I think I found the women you were looking for," Olive said appearing beside me.

I was passing the door to the main conference room. I could have hoped someone would note that I was walking with a ghost but no heads turned. In fact, it was unusually quiet in there with only the women at the registration tables who were all whispering together. Someone knew about the murder. Earlier there had been groups gathered together chatting about whatever it is that cozy mystery writers chat about.

"Where?" I asked.

"Room 673." Olive said. "They seem to be reading tarot cards. I considered appearing to them and just saying boo but I wanted to make sure they weren't the murderers first. I mean, who knows what a murderer might do when they're frightened, right?"

I smiled a bit, though as I got closer to the Skyler room, the group around Wayne looked larger and I didn't like that. Another security guard was there, putting hands down, saying something. but the women were all talking at once.

"What's going on here?" I asked in my most authoritative voice, hoping not to choke on the smell. The door to the room was still open.

A couple of the women turned. One of them was Belinda.

"Oh Maggie, you're here!" Belinda said. She looked lovely in her turquoise dress.

"What can I do?"

"We heard that Maybelle was murdered. No one had any answers at the main desk and no one would tell us where you were. I was certain you could let us know what happened?" Belinda said. Her voice held a trace of the old south. Not the Appalachian accent that many of my local workers had, but traces of something refined. I hadn't noticed the accent when she checked in but perhaps stress brought it out.

"I can't really tell you anything, other than, yes, we've had a death and I have people investigating."

Wayne looked relieved.

"There was a man behind the desk in a uniform," another woman broke in. "He said he wanted to talk to us all? He grabbed Glynis and took her into the office and we haven't seen her since."

"How long ago was that?" I asked.

"Only a few minutes ago," Nell said, pushing her way through the crowd. She'd clearly been at the fore trying to talk to Wayne or his counterpart or even pushing in to see the forensic technicians.

I nodded. "He will need to talk to everyone to try and figure out what happened. There's no need to crowd around the room. There's really nothing to see…"

"There's certainly plenty to smell," someone said.

"And we'll work on making sure it doesn't disrupt the conference," I said.

"That's not what we're worried about!" a man said, pushing forward. He was short with dark hair and glasses and looked like he might be a college professor complete with jeans and a blazer that had patches at the elbows. Had he gone out of his way to create that look?

"Yeah!" a few others echoed him.

I waited for someone to say it. The silence stretched. No one moved and it was so quiet I could hear the techs in the Skyler room moving about, their suits swooshing a bit now and then.

Finally, Belinda spoke. "I think what people aren't saying is that we're worried that there might be someone here who's a murderer."

I nodded. "I have an investigator who will want to talk to with anyone who knew the deceased or who interacted with her since she's been here. He'll want to know who might have had a reason to want to murder her. And most of all, he'll want to be sure this is done by the book, so if you know something or think you know something, you'll talk to him, alright?"

I saw heads nodding. A few arms were crossed. The professor was one with arms crossed. Belinda was nodding, along with her group. Good. At least some of them appeared to have some sense that while they might write about murder, they knew they didn't have what it took to solve a murder.

"Why don't I have each of you go upstairs and you can get started on the interview process. It's going to take some time. Due to the weather and some traffic accidents, we only have the forensic technicians and one officer," I said. I didn't add that technically Lyle was a park official, though on park land he could act as law enforcement.

Belinda was the first one to leave, heading for the elevator. She walked with a very distinct purpose and I had a feeling she just wanted to get the interview over. Her friends followed her which caused a number of others to follow behind them. Lyle wasn't going to appreciate what I'd started but I had no other ideas about how to disperse the crowd.

Several of the writers, mostly those with crossed arms, stayed behind, turning to look back into the Skyler room.

"We need you to leave the area," I repeated, as sternly as I could.

"Why?" the professor asked. "You have only one officer here and probably no more coming given that the storm is supposed to close everything down. We have experience with how criminals think."

"What sort of experience?" I asked.

"We study this in order to write our novels," he said. "Just like our detectives do."

"Are you private investigators or criminology teachers?" I asked. "Or have you consulted with your local police departments?"

It wasn't as if Lyle couldn't use the help. If someone actually had that experience, then it would be useful.

"Peggy used to work for 911," someone said.

"She's probably up in her room with her gang," another person added.

I made a mental note that Peggy might be one of the older women. Of course, who knew how many small cliques could form in a group of writers. She might not have anything to do with them. No matter, a 911 operator would have some knowledge of police procedure, but I wasn't sure she'd know enough to help Lyle. He might have to press the techs into service. At least they knew the law.

"If you don't have any specific training, then I'm afraid we won't be able to use your help. Please let our technicians work in peace," I said.

There was more grumbling but the two security guards went to work moving the writers off. When they were far enough away that none of them could get a glimpse inside the Skyler room, they started dispersing on their own.

I breathed a sigh of relief, only to turn and find Olive next to me, practically shimmering with excitement.

Chapter Ten

I walked down the hall towards the stairs and looked to see who was around. The writers were all clustered up in the lounge area near the elevators. A couple of them went into the conference room and were probably giving the people at the registration table the run down. At least Nell hadn't contacted me to demand I do something. As the conference coordinator, I'd feel more compelled to answer her inquiries to the best of my abilities than I did to the writers.

"What is it?" I asked. The open stairs near the elevators let a blast of cold air in and I shivered. Someone had opened the door upstairs. The day had really gotten cold. The only good thing was that the blast of cold air brought the faint aroma of pizza which the café would be making.

"I was watching the forensic boys in there and listening. I did appear because they weren't looking in all the corners but were focused on the body," Olive said, keeping her voice low.

"And?" I asked. I mean, I'm human. I was curious. Besides, if they had found Maybelle had perhaps fallen and hit her head, that would mean it could have been accident and I didn't have to worry—as much—about anyone else being killed.

"She was murdered with a steak knife. It's a knife like the ones in the restaurant when they serve steaks but someone had sharpened it, so they think it's premeditated," Olive said.

"Do they have prints?" I asked. If they did, the techs could probably take fingerprints from all guests, and, I hated to think it, employees, and maybe upload them to get an idea of who was at fault. That is, if the internet held out.

"Nope," Olive said. "They did find faint traces of a bit of blue fabric. They aren't sure if that was from clothing, which they said might be denim. I couldn't even see what they were talking about when they said a bit of fabric."

"It's too bad there's no a coroner to get a time of death," I said.

"They talked through the process and got a temperature. Also, given that rigor has come and gone, they believe it was longer than twelve hours ago, so sometime last night."

"I wish I'd unlocked the doors and looked inside when I came down after I heard the scream," I said. "Maybe I could have found her in time to save her."

Olive made a face. "I wonder if perhaps the woman those women saw was Maybelle's ghost rather than Maybelle herself. I mean, this place does seem to attract us."

This was another conversation Olive and I had had. People died all over the place. Hospitals should have ghosts wandering the corridors on a regular basis but no one ever reported that. Olive was of the impression that it was because these mountains were so ancient. She theorized there was some sort of energy field that held ghosts. When she pontificated on this thought, she'd add that the length of time the mountains had been around meant that more life had existed here, creating a longer chain of emotions and fears which was what created the energy field.

I'd argued that we were in the middle of nowhere. Olive argued that perhaps it hadn't always been that way. As a ghost Olive could find out a lot of things I couldn't, but one thing she couldn't do was go back in time to find out which of us was right.

"It's possible?" I said quietly, wondering. I wasn't convinced, but it would make sense if Maybelle had died *before* she went running away.

"I think that when people die suddenly, sometimes it doesn't really hit that they're dead. Perhaps she was terrified and ran," Olive said. If she'd been alive, I might have been offended by the dispassionate way she spoke of the dead, but seeing she'd been through that herself, I couldn't fault the commentary.

I nodded and pressed the button for the elevator. Olive glided into the elevator with me in her strange walking glide.

"This is terribly exciting. No one was ever murdered in the hotel when I was here. At least not that I knew of," Olive said. She sniffed a little, so I wasn't sure if she was judging me for allowing a murder or if she was disappointed. I didn't have a chance to ask her because she disappeared just before the doors opened on the first floor, lest someone was watching and noted that she was suddenly gone.

Her consideration for my guest's comfort was something I appreciated. I'd had enough of the conference writers for the moment. Many were perfectly nice people, like Belinda, but others were less so.

Upstairs, the lobby was crowded with people. Not all of them looked like writers. The young couple who had come in for a ski holiday were there, sitting near the windows, watching the snow. They were supposed to have left, but I suspected their flight was cancelled earlier today. The storm had been hitting many of the major cities in the Midwest.

Some of the others were the writers. Belinda's friends were seated over near the fireplace, their conference swag at their feet. I heard laughter from them over the general buzz of conversation around me. The room was noisier than I liked. Suzanne was back behind the desk with another desk worker. Mark was also back from searching out writers, which he'd probably found and hopefully had sent into talk to Lyle.

I slipped through the door that let me back there. "So?" I asked.

"Everyone is talking about the murder," Suzanne said. The three of them looked at me expectantly. They'd probably picked up the rumors but wanted to know what I knew.

I told them as succinctly as possible, and as quietly.

"Wow," Suzanne said. "I can't believe it. And you were down there last night and the door was locked?"

I nodded.

"I didn't notice any keys missing from the main office," Mark offered, "But if it happened later…"

Lyle would need to talk to Addy, too, although I doubted her information would be any different.

"Security has keys as well," I reminded them. "And housekeeping."

Suzanne looked up at the ceiling, probably mentally calculating all the ways someone could get a key and get into a room.

"Why the Skyler room?" she asked.

I shrugged. "It's possible someone wanted to have a quiet talk with Maybelle. Maybe they didn't mean to kill her?"

Except, of course, that was wrong. The knife that had its point and edge sharpened as Olive described suggested that the killer intended to kill. Of course, Maybelle might not have known that.

Just then, the office door opened behind us and Lyle showed Belinda out. She looked rather flushed and flustered but she made eye contact and attempted a small smile before heading out the door Lyle held for her.

I watched her hurry over to her friends and another of the women stood up.

"Did she know anything?" I asked.

"I got the general lay of the conference and how people heard about it. I also found out that she seems to know everyone and mostly likes people, but Maybelle wasn't someone she cared for," Lyle said.

"I think I saw her go out for dinner around the time I heard the scream," I said. "And other than check-in she seems to have been with her friends most of the conference."

Lyle nodded absently. He opened the door for Belinda's friend. This woman was pear shaped and wore a heavy white turtleneck over a pair of black slacks. She had on ballet flats rather than boots, so I hoped she didn't plan to head over the restaurant later this evening. A single gold chain hung around her neck. As she moved, her shoulder brown length hair parted far enough to see that she had on gold earrings of the same filigree design as the necklace.

She looked nervous as she entered the office with Lyle. I'd have loved to listen in but Lyle gave me a look before closing the door. As if I'd actually act on my desire by pressing my ear to the door, in front of Mark and Suzanne and half the hotel.

"Do you think it could happen again?" Suzanne whispered, looking around. So far, none of the people in the reception area were hurrying up to the desk to demand that we do something.

"I hope not," I said.

The thought of the publicity hit me just then. I'd been so stressed about having someone investigate and the weather that I'd not even thought about how this would play in the media. I needed to find a place to sit and work and come up with something suitably somber to post for social media, but at the moment I had nothing.

I picked up my phone, but paused to tell Mark that I would be in my apartment doing some work on the computer when a couple of the mystery writers walked by. One was a tall, thin woman with a back so straight she might have been balancing a book on her head. She wore a baggy sweater that might have better fit Belinda, over very tight leggings. Her black boots came up to her knees, but the height of the heels made them as unsuitable for the weather as the ballet flats worn by the woman Lyle was interviewing.

She was talking to heavy set bald man in a Star Trek t-shirt. He didn't appear to be cold, but at least his jeans and shoes were suitable for the weather if he put on a coat.

"Everyone hated Maybelle," she said. "And she knew it. I'm surprised she was willing to show up here after what she did to Nell on the boards."

"You know Nell was far too busy to have done anything even if she were the sort to carry a grudge," the man said. As hotel workers, we could have been furniture for all the notice they took of us.

"I think Maybelle was jealous of Belinda's following.

She doesn't have the reader fans, but she helps everyone and she's very knowledgeable," the woman continued.

"I've never liked Belinda. I think she's a phony," the man snapped. "Don't even get me started. If she were halfway fit, I'd think she murdered Maybelle, but I'm surprised she has the upper arm strength to lift a fork."

The tall woman said nothing to that. By the time she spoke, they were out of range, which was too bad. Once again, I let the appearance of being nonchalant about the whole murder thing keep me from scurrying out from behind the desk to follow the two as they spoke. Who knows what other tidbits of catty gossip I might have picked up?

Of course, I liked Belinda, far more than I liked the man, and I wanted to snap at him about weight judgements. I had a feeling confronting him about something like that wouldn't go over well in terms of professionalism. Probably good I didn't follow them to find out more.

Chapter Eleven

Back at my apartment, I had some lunch, spent time with the cats, and worked on information on my computer. I had a laptop connected to the hotel in case someone had a late-night emergency that I could solve by looking at something on the system. I didn't use it too often, but with Lyle in my office, it allowed me to get a bit of work done.

I was checking the stats for bookings for the following week to see what to order when the system blinked. The stats didn't disappear, but I noticed the internet icon had disappeared. We had the local network throughout the buildings but we were no longer connected to the outside world, at least not via the internet.

The guests might complain, particularly since, with this weather, the phones weren't likely to be much better. We did have a cell tower fairly close so we got surprisingly good service, but a storm like this could change that.

Having gotten something at least semi-productive done, I looked up who was staying in room 673, the room where Olive had noted the group of gray-haired women reading tarot cards. The room was listed under the names of Kendra and Melissa Acres. Neither of them had booked through the conference block.

I frowned. I was certain I'd seen the women with badges. I sent a note to Lyle about the fact that I didn't have them on the conference block. I hoped I wasn't giving anything away. It was possible to book outside the block and still be part of the conference, but the conference goers got a discount. We reserved a set number of rooms up until three days before. The block hadn't filled completely so even a late reservation through the block would have gotten a room.

I dug into the information a bit more, knowing I was being nosey and probably breaking our privacy policies. The women had booked three days after registration for the conference had opened.

If Olive appeared when you called her name, I'd have called her, but, as she said, she didn't often hear things when she wasn't visible. That meant, I could scream my head off for her and she wouldn't know. I used to think she was just stubborn about doing what she wanted. I'd need to reevaluate that based on what I'd learned. You'd think in all our years together, becoming friends, that she would have mentioned what she could and could not do in more detail.

Then again, perhaps what she could and could not do as a ghost felt personal or made her feel vulnerable in some way. Not that I was a ghost hunter or anything. Still, she hadn't known me in life. While I'd think the dead would be braver, this was another thing Olive and I had never discussed.

I sighed. Olive had seen two other women in the room. Maybe I'd been mistaken and only two of the women were part of the writer's group? But I was sure I'd seen the lanyards on all the women, despite the fact that the registration table hadn't officially opened. Several others had gotten their writer information as well, so I knew that the women having lanyards wasn't suspicious, unless they weren't actually part of the conference.

I attempted a search on their names, wondering if I'd find a website with books, but of course, nothing happened. The internet was down. I sighed.

I made a few notes, in case Lyle asked more questions. I rubbed Latte's head and gave Chai a chin rub and then left them snoozing on the afghan. They looked annoyed that there wasn't any sun. I glanced out the back window, noting that snow was sticking to the tree branches out back as well as the ground. A large limb that had been hanging low on one of the trees had already fallen. I hoped more didn't come down. All the trees were well out of range of the hotel but I loved my view and hated it when one of my trees came down and changed it.

Now, I needed to check in with my staff managers to make sure they had everything they thought they would need.

I looked at the weather app on my phone. Of course, I had to wait a very long time. I wondered if anything was going to happen, but finally, I got some numbers. Everything looked much the same as earlier. The snow was still expected to continue well into the night. There continued to be blizzard warnings for our area, though I had no idea if that was still from this morning or if it was the most updated information. Given how slow I had gotten the information, I didn't push it and figured I'd always be able to look outside and see what was happening.

I used the staff elevator, and it wasn't long before I was upstairs. I stopped first at the front desk.

"Anything?" I asked Mark.

"We had one of our guests return because they

couldn't get out of town," Mark said. "We'd already turned over their room to someone else, but I shifted things around and they're in one of the empty mini-suites. Their check out time was fairly early, so I hope no one else has to come back. We've had two people add an extra day, and I've gotten the writers their rooms for the conference."

"Did you mark out a room for the forensic investigators?" I asked.

"I did," Mark said. "It's one on the second floor near the freight elevator. Hopefully they won't notice too much."

"Two beds?" I asked.

Mark gave a nod.

"Well, if someone isn't here and they don't have a reservation, they can't just show up and assume we have openings. Make sure that our street sign shows we're booked, not that it matters as we don't get drive-by traffic. If we get a moment of internet, make sure to update our booking status there. Even if we have some free rooms, I don't want people trying to get here with this weather."

"Already done, even before the internet went down. I didn't want someone thinking they could just pull off the highway and expect to find a room," Mark said. "The dorms are full and with the conference, even the downstairs public rooms are in use. We've got a handful of rooms, but other than that, about the only place we have to put people would be in the reception area and mezzanine if there's an emergency."

"I ordered plenty of food. I know people at conferences and conventions always bring their appetites."

"Darnell called up and he said the fuel supplies for the generators look good. They were serviced two weeks ago," Mark added.

"I talked to him yesterday," I said. I shook my head a little, thinking about our janitorial manager.

Darnell worried that because he worked in janitorial services down in the sub-basement that we thought he didn't do anything. I knew he worked harder than most of us. I'd seen less of him than I'd seen of most of our ghosts in the years I'd been here. Darnell was one of the few employees who had been with the hotel longer than I had. If I didn't know better, I'd have thought he was a ghost. Or some sort of hotel legend, just a voice on the phone at least once a week to give a report on what he thought might need to be fixed.

Mark smiled a knowing smile. We were all used to Darnell's worries.

The office door opened behind us. A man I hadn't seen before stepped out and left the area once Lyle pointed to the exit.

"How's it going?" I asked.

"Fifteen interviews down. They're getting a bit shorter because I have certain information that seems to get repeated and I'm not clarifying that as much," Lyle said.

"Can we do anything?" I asked.

"I got your email with the names of those women. I haven't interviewed them yet and I'd like to. Do you think you could phone up there? I just asked my last interview to grab someone else, but I should be free in a few," Lyle said. "I got a note from the forensics techs. They're finishing up. Your security people have been helpful as far as getting them a transport for the body and finding a place to put it. Your off-premises storage shed should be plenty cold for our purposes."

I nodded. That would be far easier than having to clean up one of the walk-ins after having had a body in it.

I picked up my cell and called to let people know they didn't have to move all the food.

"Do we need a guard?" I asked.

Lyle sighed. "Ideally, but I'm not going to force anyone to stand outside in this weather. Even inside the shed, it's going to be cold. That's the whole point."

"I'll make sure we have someone patrol at least once an hour," I said.

Mark didn't even look as he picked up the hotel phone and punched the button for the security office.

"Great," Lyle said.

A tiny woman who looked more like an eight year old than an adult pushed open the door. Behind her was the man who had just left. The woman had a lanyard with the conference information on it, so she was definitely a writer. Closer, I noted that her face was lined. She was just short and slender, and wearing her pale blonde hair in a ponytail made her look younger than her years.

"Come on back," Lyle said, holding a hand out to the office.

I watched her go inside and waited until the door closed. Then I used the phone to call up to room 673. I listened to it ring. And ring. No answer. I hung up without leaving a message. Silly, but I didn't want to warn anyone that they were wanted for questioning.

"I'll go take a tour of the premises and see who needs what," I said. I left Mark and Suzanne to the front desk and headed over to the stairs. I'd have a better chance of seeing more people going down the stairs than I would in an elevator. My feet protested, but only a little. I was used to walking the premises a dozen times a day.

I passed a small group of people laughing, going upstairs. I noticed only one of them had on a lanyard. I frowned. Did writers bring family with them to these things? Did that impact the questions about Maybelle? She'd been alone in her room. I knew that because I'd checked her in. Even if I hadn't checked her in, giving her only one key card at her request, I couldn't imagine her sharing a room.

Lyle really ought to go up there and search. I had't even thought about it until now, which meant there was a good chance the maids had already done their work. I turned around and headed back up to the desk.

"Fastest walk-through ever," Mark said quietly.

I shook my head, smiling. I picked up the phone to buzz housekeeping.

"Housekeeping. This is Pamela," the voice said. Pamela had the faintest trace of an Eastern European accent. If I didn't live in the south, I probably wouldn't have noticed but her words were slightly more clipped even than mine.

"Pamela, can you see if room 491 has been cleaned yet?" I asked. Maybelle's room looked over the mountains rather than the parking lot, though anything above the second floor had a decent view of the landscape around us.

"It's not checked off yet," Pamela said.

"I need housekeeping to avoid that room, okay?" I said.

"I'll call her," Pamela said and hung up.

I hoped that was enough. I logged on the local network and typed a note to let Lyle know that I had stopped housekeeping in Maybelle's room. I gave him the room number.

He opened the office door and the woman left, scurrying, which at her tiny size made me think of a rodent.

"Are the women you located here?" he asked.

"I tried calling, but no one answered. They may have left for lunch. I was going to go walk around and look for them when I realized that you or the techs might want to look at Maybelle's room. I just asked housekeeping not to clean it."

Lyle nodded. He ran a hand through is hair and nodded again, thinking. "Maybe it's a good time to take a break from interviews. I'm getting things mixed up in my mind. I can look through her room, maybe grab a coke and then get back to it. If you locate the women, that would be great. It seems like they were the ones most likely to have seen the vic last."

I bit back a smile at Lyle's use of the word "vic." He normally used names, but I knew he was trying to act like what he thought of as a "real" police officer.

"I'll take you up," I said.

This time, I headed towards the elevators rather than the stairs. I didn't need to meet anyone, at least not right then. I whispered to Mark about Kendra and Melissa Acres and their room number. He could watch for any charges to their room and let me know where they had been made when I came back down.

Chapter Twelve

Lyle and I got off the elevator on the fourth floor to the sound of laughter from one of the guest rooms across the way. A housekeeping cart was a few doors up from Maybelle's room. I'd gotten to housekeeping just in time.

"If someone could get into the Skyler room, they could probably get into Maybelle's room," Lyle said. "Forensics didn't mention finding a room key on her, although they might not have considered that immediately important. I'll have their report on all findings in an hour or so."

"The conference room masters are different from the room masters. Only the managers have a true master key that opens anything," I said. "It's to make sure guests have a bit more privacy and safety."

Lyle didn't make a note of that. It might not be important if Maybelle's room key wasn't on her person. If it was, well, he'd remember, or I'd remind him.

I opened the door and started to step in, but Lyle put a hand out to hold me back while he entered alone. It smelled faintly of cigarettes, though smoking wasn't allowed in the hotel. I hated it when people ignored that, particularly since I probably couldn't add the charge to Maybelle's credit card after her death.

The sound of canned television laughter from another hotel room reached me. I thought it came from upstairs. It felt wrong to be listening to such happy sounds when I was standing outside a dead woman's room.

"I looked in here earlier, when I was looking for the gray-haired women." Olive said, appearing beside me. If I wasn't so used to her doing that, I'd have jumped. "It was a mess, then, too."

I leaned further into the room, noting that the covers of the king-sized bed were in a wad on the floor. The desk drawer was open. No one had damaged the television, though it was at an awkward angle for watching and housekeeping had instructions to make sure it was flat against the wall. Lyle was examining a side table.

"Did you notice anything?" I asked.

"Just that it was a mess," Olive said. "You didn't tell me it was her room. Don't tell me in all this time you haven't figured out that some people are pigs?"

Working in hotels you ran into all kinds. People who kept the room so tidy that housekeeping barely had to clean toilets. There were others who left everything out and spills everywhere. I didn't envy the workers who had to clean in most of the rooms.

I heard the snap of Lyle's camera, so I knew he was taking more photos. Forensics would need to get in there.

"If the victim wasn't a slob," Olive said, "and at this point, that's an if, then someone was looking very hard for something. I wonder what she could have had that was so important."

I tried to think of something a writer might have that another writer would want. An award would have a name on it. Manuscripts were typically on computers.

"Lyle, is there a laptop in there?" I asked. "Or was there one downstairs?"

"Nothing downstairs. She did have her phone," Lyle said. "I'm not seeing a laptop in here but I'm leaving most of this for forensics. You think she had information on someone?"

"I'm thinking maybe she stole someone else's work? Or someone wanted to steal her work," I said. "She's a writer. That seems like the most logical thing for someone to steal." Not to mention I'd just read a thriller about a writer who wrote a book much like a crime an acquaintance had committed. The acquaintance was sure he was the criminal in the book and had been chasing the writer for the manuscript that sat on his computer. It had been very exciting.

Lyle stared at me for a moment. He shook his head, but I could see that he was filing that information away. Lyle was good at figuring things out. He might not be a reader, might not think like a reader or a writer, but he wasn't a fool. Anything could be valuable to someone.

"I've got my photos. Lock this up and make sure your housekeeper knows to skip this room," he said.

I turned and locked the room and then spoke to the maid on duty on this floor. She'd already gotten word and wouldn't go into the room. I also asked her to let me know if anyone else went into the room. If forensics came up here, I'd have to let them in, so no one but me ought to be trying to get in there.

Then I hurried to catch up to Lyle who was nearly at the elevator.

"Did anyone suggest that someone might be copying her work?" I asked.

Lyle gave me a look and sighed. "You know I can't talk about the interviews."

"This is hotel business in a way. We're all stuck here with a murderer for at least the next couple of days," I said.

"Join me in the office and I'll tell you what I can. It won't be everything, but hopefully, it will give you some peace of mind. And we can figure out what to tell guests who might be distressed," he said.

Getting off the elevator, I caught sight of the gray-haired women that Lyle wanted to interview. One had on a beautiful blue sweater. I wondered about the fabric that Olive had said had been found near the body.

"Those two women were two of the women I saw downstairs when I heard the scream, yesterday," I said, pointing. I didn't mention the scrap of fabric. Olive had given me that information. I had no idea if Lyle had it, but it wasn't up to me to tell him. And he might be annoyed that Olive was listening in and expect me to do something about it. As if anyone could tell Olive anything.

Lyle quickened his pace to catch up. "Excuse me!" he called. One of the women turned, frowning. She had her badge on her lanyard. I couldn't believe she hadn't heard about the murder.

Lyle spoke to her but the music and the conversations kept me from hearing. I saw her shake her head and then point at her friend. Lyle persisted. Neither of the women looked pleased. They glanced at each other.

Lyle stayed there staring at them. Finally, one of them broke off and headed towards the desk with him and the other left to head towards the café, though it was in that late afternoon time when it wasn't lunch but not yet time for dinner.

I sighed. So much for getting the low down on what was going on.

Chapter Thirteen

I headed back towards the front desk more slowly than Lyle. Mark was still there but Suzanne was gone. Another one of my front desk people stood there with him, typing on the computer, his fingers hitting the keyboard so hard, I could hear the click of the keys even over the music.

I slipped through the door behind Lyle and the woman. Lyle glanced at me his eyebrows furrowing as if he worried I thought we'd still meet to talk. I broke off and went to talk to Mark.

"Have any of the guests asked about Maybelle?" I asked them.

"A couple," Mark said. "Both writers, and I referred them to Nell."

"Does Nell know anything?" I asked.

"If she does, we haven't told her," Mark said. "I don't know anything to tell her other than the woman is dead and we have investigators here."

I nodded. "We need to come up with something to tell people that sounds decent. And I should find Nell to try and coordinate what we ought to tell people about Maybelle. I'm sure she'll want to make an announcement."

Checking the computer, I found Nell's information. I called the room on the house phone but there was no answer. I tried her cell using mine and was unsurprised to find there was no service. Given how long it had taken for the weather app to come up earlier, I should have realized it wouldn't work. Cell phones would be down until the storm blew over. Another thing for guests to complain about.

I glared at the windows that were still swirled with ice. Glancing out the large glass doors, I noted that the snowflakes were smaller and there were more of them. We only had one bellhop near the front and he looked bored.

"She's probably down in the main conference room," I said, referring to Nell.

"She'll probably let the writers know that Maybelle died," Mark said. "After all, Maybelle was one of them. Most probably know already, so not mentioning it would be in poor taste."

I nodded, mentally noting that. "I think when people ask, we do need to say that yes, a guest was found dead in one of the conference rooms and the police are looking into what happened. That's general enough and leaves room for them to think it's an accident rather than a murder, okay?"

Mark nodded. "About what I was telling people anyway."

"Then we're on the same page."

I left them at the desk, looking longingly over my shoulder at my office door. I wanted to know what Lyle knew. Maybe that would help me with Nell. I took the stairs, surprised to find quite a few writers milling around outside the main conference room. A few heads turned as I crossed the room, looking at me suspiciously, I thought. Or perhaps that was just my imagination.

A different security guard sat outside the Skyler room, so Wayne must have either finished his shift or gone on break. No writers were down there trying to talk to her. Good.

I poked my head into the conference room. Nell was near the registration table, looking through a box.

"Nell," I said.

She practically jumped when I said her name.

"Sorry," she said, smoothing down her blouse. She wore slacks and solid black walking shoes and a blazer over a navy blue sweater. It seemed that blue, unfortunately, was a popular color. Her hair was lightly mussed but not bad. Her cheeks were pinker than normal but she could have been working hard.

"Is now a bad time?" I hoped that she would say no and would talk to me.

Fortunately, the light in Nell's eyes suggested she was as eager to head off somewhere and chat as I was.

"Not at all." Nell looked back at the three writers at the table. I noticed the professorial man was one of them. He didn't look as if he approved of her talking to me.

"Let's head somewhere quiet," I said. I took Nell towards the Skylar room.

"We're not going into the room where Maybelle…" she whispered.

"No, but it's quiet and I have a security guard to keep anyone from listening," I said.

Nell nodded. "Thank heavens. I know I'm supposed to go and talk to the officer upstairs but it's been a madhouse of questions. Maybelle was supposed to lead a panel so I had to cancel it and I'm scrambling to add something to the program. Two of our other speakers didn't get in before the storm."

"What about having a vigil for Maybelle?"

Nell gave a bark of laughter. "No one would come."

"She was that unpopular?" Nell definitely needed to talk to Lyle but I wasn't going to pass up the chance to find out what I could.

"You don't know the half of it. Cheryl Richards is a past president of the society and Maybelle made a big stink that Cheryl had plagiarized one of her books, although the accusation was ridiculous. Even went to court last year, finally, and it was tossed out," Nell said. "That didn't win Maybelle any friends. And her personality wasn't exactly the sort that made people feel like being very forgiving."

"Is Cheryl here?" I asked.

"She was one of the people who didn't make it. I think she got to Charlotte last night but had no way to get any further," Nell said.

Interesting.

"Is there anyone who had a particular reason to dislike Maybelle?"

"Not any more than anyone else. Maybelle was a prima dona and a pain in the ass—forgive my French," Nell said.

"Do most writers travel with laptops or tablets?" I figured this was a general enough question.

"Definitely," Nell said. "You want to be able to write, or at least jot down notes and plenty of people just take notes on their electronics now."

"Up at the front desk we're just telling people that Maybelle died and that the police are looking into her death. If you make an announcement, could you stick to something like that?" I asked.

"I can, although to be honest, I doubt I need to make

an announcement. Just about every writer here has a theory of how she died," Nell said.

"What's yours?" I asked, smiling a little.

"I think Maybelle accused the wrong person of stealing an idea and they weren't willing to have the public legal battle. Or didn't have the funds. Some of our indie writers don't make a ton of money and couldn't afford to defend themselves against her," Nell said.

"Anyone with a temper or temperament to do that?" Lyle wouldn't be pleased to hear this conversation but I was grabbing my moment.

Nell sighed. "I think given the right motivation just about anyone here would probably at least consider killing Maybelle. I mean, she's so generally disliked that I could see a *Murder on the Orient Express* situation where everyone here took a shot at killing her and no one knows which was the cause of death."

I hadn't read the book, but I had seen the movie. I hoped it held true to the general story. Lyle would hate that theory.

"Ed, the guy in the blazer who looks like a 1960s English professor," Nell began, making me laugh a bit. "He thinks it was Melissa Acres."

Now there was a name I'd heard before.

"Does he say why?" I asked, trying not to act too eager. I wondered if Lyle was interviewing Melissa right then.

Nell gave a small sigh. "It's convoluted. Melissa and Kendra are sisters who co-write cozy mysteries about two old women who are cousins living in assisted living. Maybelle hated the books and has given them bad reviews on all the sites. She's very specific about the things she's thinks are problems. There are rumors that she has multiple profiles on some of the sites so that she can review more than once. The reviews have kept Melissa and

Kendra from getting some types of advertising that require a certain average of star reviews. And, of course, it's possible that the low review scores might have turned off other buyers."

That didn't sound convoluted at all. "It seems like a reasonable thing to think they dislike her. Is there a reason they might have murdered her?" As if losing money wasn't enough. Maybe the sisters were desperate?

"That's the thing. Despite that, their books sell well within a certain niche of readers. Those readers probably don't even look at the reviews and just see another book of the sort they like. No, it's more that Maybelle has tried to blackball them from the mystery writing groups. It hasn't worked, but I know the two always worry that she'll find a way to succeed. They didn't even register through the block of rooms to save money because they were so worried someone might be Maybelle's friend and let her know they'd be here. Maybelle has been known to prepare quite long speeches about people she doesn't like, particularly if she knows they'll be around to hear her make them." Nell shook her head.

"We'd have shut her down, of course, but the psychological damage gets done. No amount of friends and support helps when someone seems to have a vendetta against you, particularly when it seems like it's there for no apparent reason," Nell went on.

That was a bit more convoluted, but I could see why the two women would be suspects. And the fact that they were downstairs when there was a scream was also suspect.

"I would think that knowing no one particularly liked Maybelle would have helped," I said.

"We all have our little things that are sort of anti-Maybelle, but most of us have just had little things. Maybelle had an active vendetta against the sisters. I think that's what made it so hard for them. Some people would have laughed it off and said, her problem, but Kendra, especially, is terribly shy. She's not a social person at all. She and Melissa have a few closer friends that they'll socialize with, but that's about it. Kendra won't even come to the larger events like tonight's social or tomorrow's opening. She'll do the breakout sessions with Melissa and that's all anyone will see of her."

I wasn't a psychologist to be able to determine if that made it more likely that Melissa would harm Maybelle or if Kendra would take on the task herself. But it would give Kendra an alibi if she missed a friendly chat. Melissa could easily cover for her saying she was overwhelmed. Heck, Kendra could probably even convince her sister that she was overwhelmed.

"What do you think?" I asked.

"I can't imagine Kendra hurting anyone. She's the sort that would break down crying if confronted. I think Maybelle might have gotten to her once and that may be what started the vendetta. The fact that she could easily hurt someone probably made her feel powerful," Nell said.

"Melissa is kind but she's short and she's not particularly strong. I can't imagine her having the strength to murder someone."

I'd have to check and see how long the sisters had been at the hotel. Someone had to go to the restaurant and sharpen a knife. I'd look up to see how long that would take. At the very least, it seemed like it would require special tools to file the tip to sharpness at least. But I wasn't a knife expert.

"Who would you pick?" I asked.

Nell shook her head. "We might write about murder, but no one here is exactly murderous, you know? Jerry jokes about it, but that's about it."

"Someone makes a joke about killing people?" I repeated.

Nell smiled. "No. He just jokes that he could kill someone because he's thought up all the good ways of doing it."

That made sense. I could see that.

"But no one here is really mean. At least not that I've noticed in previous conferences or online. Heated arguments, but most people back down if someone says they're getting out of line," Nell said. She frowned, clearly thinking.

I waited, hoping she'd share whatever it was she was considering.

But then she shook her head and looked at me. "I guess I'll be up there just saying what you suggested. While everyone thinks that Maybelle was murdered, no need to go advertising the fact."

I smiled as well, wishing I knew what she'd been thinking of. I started down the hallway, only to feel the chill of an imminent Clara appearance. I moved to the side of the hall so she didn't run through me and give me a major chill.

Nell didn't move and when Clara appeared and ran down the hall, she ran right through Nell, causing her to double over and gasp. It made me wonder if perhaps Clara was what had caused Maybelle to scream and perhaps give herself away to the women sitting downstairs.

But that situation would be a crime of opportunity. It was unlikely that someone taking advantage of that moment would just happen to have a sharpened knife on them.

Chapter Fourteen

I left Nell and went back upstairs. Lyle ought to be done talking with the women soon enough. I could let him know what I'd learned from Nell. My questions would probably be different from his. And as far as suggesting suspects, she was far less likely to tell someone official. She and I could be innocently gossiping.

As I reached the reception area, I immediately noticed the noise level upstairs was higher. It was still afternoon, though it was so dark it might have been evening with the low clouds and ice-covered windows. Looking out through the glass doors, I thought if I went out there, I'd disappear as soon as I left the portico. I could barely make out the large bus that the forensics officers had left under there.

The chairs in the reception area were all crowded around the big fireplace and a large group of men and women were all talking. Frank, the ghost hunter was there. He and a couple of other guests were talking with the writers, who all had on their lanyards and badges. I hoped they weren't all talking about murder. We didn't need more guests adding fuel to the gossip.

I noticed they had drinks from the bar which appeared to be hopping, though the music was still low. When I glanced up at the mezzanine, people were seated up there as well, though it seemed like they were in smaller groups.

Having surveyed this part of my domain, I hurried back to the front desk. A younger desk worker was there alone.

"Where's Mark?" I asked.

"He's off on a break," he said. "He said he needed to go sit down for a moment."

That meant Mark could be anywhere, from a quiet spot in the upstairs bar, to the restaurant, which was probably fairly quiet right now. It was that awkward time where it was a little too early for drinking, though clearly not for all guests, but too late for eating lunch. Hopefully, he took one of our local area network pagers so we could contact him if needed.

The door to my office opened and another gray-haired woman stepped out. I thought it might be one of the women, though not one of the more noticeable ones, from downstairs. She had on a brown sweater, though her jeans were quite blue. Lyle breathed out.

"You have a minute?" I asked.

He gestured to me to come in. I wasn't sure how I felt about him feeling so comfortable in my office that he felt he could gesture me in.

I closed the door after me and took a seat in one of the guest chairs again. I didn't like it any more than I had earlier.

"Well?" I asked.

"Not getting much," he said. "Maybelle had tangled with a few people legally, mostly about her writing or their writing, rather, claiming they had plagiarized her work."

"The one person I heard about that happening to, isn't at the conference," I said.

"Cheryl something, wasn't it?"

"I think so," I said.

"Yeah. I guess Maybelle also went after some guy named Ashford Lowell," Lyle said. "He shut her down pretty quickly. Guess he doesn't write cozies. He's into the thriller category. Indie published and the rumor was that Maybelle hoped to make some money having him pay her because he'd be afraid to hire an attorney."

"I heard that Maybelle harassed Melissa and Kendra Acres quite a bit," I said.

"Heard that too. In fact, that was Melissa you just saw. Kendra was here earlier. They have two good friends that they've been hanging out with, but the four of them alibi each other. They said they saw Maybelle running just like they told you but hadn't seen her later. According to Kendra and another one of their friends, the group left shortly after seeing Maybelle to go up to their room to try and commune with the spirits of the hotel." Lyle made a face.

"I'll ask Olive if they succeeded," I said with a straight face.

Lyle just stared. He knew that Olive and I talked. He'd seen her more than once, but there was something about admitting to seeing ghosts that bothered him. I supposed if our situations were reversed, I might feel the same way.

"I don't like that they seem to be the last ones to see her," Lyle said.

"Or at least admit to it," I said. "And they couldn't help admitting to it because I saw them. I wondered, and you'll forgive me for getting all woo-woo, but could they have seen Maybelle's ghost? Maybe someone had already murdered her?"

Lyle rolled his eyes but then he sighed. "In this hotel, I can't rule anything out. At least not until we get the coroner. I hope that shed stays cold enough."

"The last weather report I got was that it was supposed to stay quite cold for several days after the snow stops. Someone should be able to get through and pick her up and she shouldn't be too decomposed."

"I wish cell service hadn't gone down. I thought we paid for that extra tower up over there to make sure it didn't," Lyle complained.

"We did. In fact, this is the first time it's gone out since the tower was put up four years ago. Before that, we'd lose service if the sky got overcast," I reminded him.

"Anything else?" he asked.

"I talked to Nell and asked her what the writers thought," I said. I gave him the comments on Melissa and Kendra, the comments I heard about Belinda, and also Nell's comment on someone named Jerry Benson.

"I haven't talked to him. Can't see Belinda doing it. She seems soft," Lyle said. "And more likely to talk someone to death than murder them."

"I liked her, so I hope it's not her."

Lyle humphed at that.

"I think that Nell knew something more. Or she thought of something but didn't want to tell me," I said. "I doubt that if it's speculation, she'll tell you, but I want you to know that there's something she's holding back. It might be nothing more than a rumor that someone else tells you, but still…"

"I'll be sure to press," Lyle said. "She knows she's supposed to come see me?"

He looked up when someone rapped on the door.

"Yes?" Lyle bellowed. I would have gotten up to open it

and not yelled. That was something I found very irritating about Lyle. He tended to be noisy.

"It's a Jerry Benson here to talk to you," the desk worker called.

"Send him in," Lyle said. Then looking at me, eyebrows raised. "Speak of the devil."

"Indeed." I made no move to get up, hoping that I'd be allowed to stay but Lyle glared at me as Jerry came in. I sighed and pushed myself out of my chair to go back to work, though I really wanted to know what Jerry had to say for himself.

I passed Jerry, noting that he was older than I had pictured him, white hair pulled back in a short ponytail, a barrel-shaped body with a broad chest, but arms that looked thinner than they should be. The button-down shirt he wore had frayed edges at the cuffs as if it had been worn to death. The blue trousers were also looking a bit threadbare. It was certainly possible that they had left the small scrap of blue fabric behind, though I saw nothing obvious. I wondered if he still wore the items because he didn't want to shop or if his finances were such that he couldn't afford a new shirt or pants.

I tried to notice everything because I wanted to know more about him, particularly if he were being mentioned as a possible murderer, though he wasn't any more likely to have killed Maybelle than anyone else. But, it was my job, after all, to keep my guests safe.

Chapter Fifteen

Later that day, well into evening, I was back in my apartment. I had the gas fireplace on and the cats curled in front of it enjoying the heat it put out. I had the lights off so I could watch the snow falling. The Inn's outside lights allowed me to do so. It was coming down so hard sometimes all I saw was white. This was definitely going to be a storm for the record books.

I'd been hearing about that for some days, but you never really believe until it's there and you're in the middle of it. I had no television because it relied on cable, which was out. The guests probably weren't pleased, though Nell had indicated that she'd brought a bunch of movies on DVD to show in the main room. With any luck she'd started early.

We did have a supply of DVDs and I hoped that the reception area bar was using them to show something interesting on the big television there.

Other than the occasional snort from Chai, who has a tendency to snore, the apartment was quiet. It smelled faintly of the chicken soup I'd made for my dinner, along with a piece of thick French bread that I'd added garlic and parmesan to. It was more than enough given how stressed I felt. Normally, I'd be reading on an evening like this. Tonight, I couldn't concentrate.

The one good thing about the snow was that it was rather mesmerizing. So there I sat, on the plump cushions of my sofa, my feet stretched out in front of me, the afghan my cats loved covering my legs, not quite meditating and certainly not dozing but ruminating upon the questions of the day.

I nearly jumped out of my skin when the apartment phone rang. My cell would have been the usual method of communication but without cell service, someone had to use the main phones. The ringer on that was far too loud for my taste. Latte and Chai didn't exactly like it either, both of them leaping to their feet and then running for the bedroom, as if the phone was going to let someone into their home.

Calming my heart rate down, I got up and went over to the phone that still hung on the wall on that separated the kitchen from the hallway. It was easily accessed from the living room, which was, no doubt, why it was there.

"What's up?" I asked. Anyone calling on this number had to be from the front desk and knew they were calling me.

"Kendra Acres is at the front desk and can't locate her sister Melissa. The writers have looked everywhere around the hotel. We had security on the lookout for her and she appears to have disappeared," Addy said. "I know there's nothing you can do, but I figured you'd need to be notified."

"Has Lyle been told?" I asked.

"I'm not sure where he is or how to get a hold of him," Addy said.

"If he's not in my office, he's probably in one of the dorms, or else eating. We need to get him one of our walkies so we can always get a hold of him," I said. I made a mental note to do that.

"Should I have security go looking for him?" Addy asked.

"Yes, please. Start with the dorms here. I'll be up in a few," I said. Addy might be right that there wasn't anything I could do to speed the discovery of a missing patron but it looked better to have the manager on duty.

In the bedroom, I slipped out of my flannel nightshirt with regret and pulled on a pair of blue jeans and a sweater. The jeans were more casual than I usually went but it was after hours and I was not supposed to be working. I was only willing to forgo the comfort of my relaxation clothing so far to find someone.

As I hurried down the hall, I realized it would be easy enough for me to poke my head into the dorm down there and see if I could find Lyle. Opening the long door to the men's dorm, I hoped that no one was in the middle of changing. It already smelled of old socks and glancing down the room, half the bunks were unmade. A couple of people were sleeping.

I saw no one sitting up doing work. I doubted that Lyle was one of the mounds snoring simply because he hadn't had to be up quite as early as some of my shift workers, who were probably the sleepers. It was barely eight.

I hurried out, passing the women's dorm, knowing Lyle wouldn't have bunked in there by mistake. He didn't have a key for any of the private areas beyond the dorm, so chances were, he'd have to be in a public area. The only other place he might have taken refuge was the room I'd put the forensic techs in. There was room in there for a cot if needed. Housekeeping would know.

Upstairs, more people milled about than I expected. Music came from the bar and I did see shadows of movement from the big TV. I didn't go over to see what they'd chosen.

"Anything?" I asked when I got to the front desk. Addy was there on her own, at least for the moment.

Addy shook her head. "Kendra went back to the room, finally. She seemed really anxious."

"I heard she has some social anxiety. I bet she's lost without her sister." I logged onto the computer and found the room the techs were staying in. I called up there.

"Yo?" a male voice said.

"This is Maggie, the manager down at the front desk. You didn't happen to squeeze Lyle into your room, did you?"

A slight chuckle. "We would have if you'd given us a suite, but he's only here to go over what we've learned," the man said. "You need him?"

"Please," I said.

The phone was turned over to Lyle.

"What is it?"

"Kendra Acres was down here. Apparently, she can't find her sister Melissa. Addy tells me they had security searching for her. Nell had the writers on the lookout, but no one has seen her." I hoped my voice didn't shake. Security would have opened the rooms and looked for her. No reason for me to go searching in the locked conference rooms.

Lyle sighed. "I'll be right down. Hopefully, she's just moving around the hotel and security has missed her. You have cameras?"

"Of course we do," I said. "And they're on. I'm sure security looked on those first."

Because that would be the process if she were a child.

A security person would start the walk and another would look at the cameras to find a child. No reason an adult wouldn't be treated any differently. On a normal day, we'd have figured an adult had left the property and left it up to the person to contact the authorities to see what they said. In this storm, however, I doubted that Melissa would be going anywhere.

"Did someone check the parking lot?" Lyle asked.

I sighed. "I'll talk to security. Have them send someone up here to confer with you."

Hanging up, I looked at Addy.

"Do you know if we sent anyone out to the parking lot?" I asked.

"Kendra said they didn't ride in their car. They came with their friends. Melissa wouldn't have a key and both of their friends said she hadn't asked for one." Addy looked down at some notes. "I think Jake went out to the portico and shined a flashlight around, but there were no footprints leaving that area. He walked down through the covered walk to the restaurant and looked for footprints or something obvious but there wasn't anything."

Which meant it was unlikely that anyone had gone out there. Of course, the way snow was falling, that could have obscured any footprints. Even so, I wasn't sending security to search the lot in this mess. While it was cold, it wasn't Antarctica, but the snow was heavy enough that visibility was low and getting lost wouldn't be good. Besides, given the way so many of our guests were dressed, I hoped that Melissa hadn't gone out. It might not be the kind of cold that can kill you in a few minutes, but in a few hours of wandering...that would be another story.

Lyle was down in almost no time. "Well?"

Jake hurried out of the main elevator. He was still

dressed in a bright red vest over his heavy down jacket. Light snow flaked on the shoulders.

"Jake?" I said, nodding at Lyle.

"No sign of her," Jake said. "I've got someone looking at the cameras that may pick her up. We don't have them in the rooms, so if she's with someone, we wouldn't know. I woke up one of the early shifters to look through tapes since around six, which was when she went to dinner with her sister. They ate in the café. I checked around the sides of the restaurant and then went up to the mezzanine to see if I could see anything outside through those windows, but they're just as iced up as the ones down here. Worse."

Lyle nodded. "Any signs outside?"

Jake shook his head. "In addition to how hard it's snowing, we've had periodic wind gusts, so footprints would have been erased. I didn't see any lights that didn't make sense or movement that didn't seem right. The flashlights we've got are pretty strong and I had Angie, at the door, turn on all the floodlights."

"Why aren't they always on?" Lyle asked. "Seems like that would be safer in this weather."

"No one's out driving," Jake said. "Or they shouldn't be. And we're on generator power, so we need to conserve what we can. The floods are hooked up to the generators because normally we'd only need them for about a day. This is expected to last several days."

Lyle nodded. "Her sister saw her last around six?"

"They probably spent until seven in the café," Jake said. "Receipt signed by Melissa, charged to their room, says nine minutes after seven. Kendra says they went straight up to their room. When they got there, Melissa said she was going to find a soda. She left and hasn't been back."

"And she checked with friends and the other writers but no one has seen her?" Lyle clarified.

Jake nodded.

Lyle sighed. He glanced out towards the doors, his shoulders slumping. As a park ranger, pushed into being a detective, a part of him would probably feel more comfortable outside searching, even in this. The other part of him probably knew better than any of us what we might find.

"And you did a search?" Lyle asked.

Jake nodded.

"Did you unlock the locked conference rooms and any employee only areas?" Lyle asked.

"I did. I didn't look in places like the walk-ins because there are people in all the kitchens. Someone would have seen someone dragging a person in there. Besides, with the number of people we have around, chances are someone would have found her by now."

"What about the shed?" I asked.

"I'm not even sure how she'd know to go out there," Jake said. "I can send someone, but it might take a bit."

The shed was down a fairly steep hill, even going out the back of the hotel. In the dark and in this weather, it wouldn't be particularly safe.

"That would be dangerous in this weather," I added, glancing at Lyle to see what he'd say.

Lyle rolled his eyes. "Shit. I'll get my gear and go out there. Get me a map so I can take a look. And if you have a really long rope, that'd be good. If I remember correctly, nothing I have is quite long enough."

He hurried off to the employee elevator, probably to get any gear he might have stashed in one of the dorms.

I made eye contact with Jake who strode after him. Security had a lot of storage down in the sub-basement. I hoped that Melissa wasn't outside. I couldn't think of a good reason for her to have gone out, either. It was too bad the men had to be thorough. It was definitely not safe to be wandering around. At least Lyle wanted rope, which I assumed would anchor him to the main part of the Inn.

"Did you ask Kendra what Melissa was wearing when she left?" I asked Addy.

Addy looked down at her notes. "A heavy pink and white sweater and blue jeans. She had on boots, but they weren't snow boots."

No one in their right mind would have gone out to search for the shed dressed like that, even if they knew exactly how to get there. It wasn't like our storage facilities were on maps for guests so they could go hang out with the tarps and extra petrol.

"So she didn't appear to be planning to go outside," I said. "Which means she almost has to be in someone's room."

"What about Maybelle's room?" Addy asked.

I gave her a long look. No one else would be in there. If the forensics technicians had gone through the room, it would be empty. Even if they hadn't, someone could easily get in and out of there quickly.

I hurried up the stairs to the mezzanine, planning to catch the elevator there. I glanced around, looking for writers. They were scattered around downstairs but not as many were upstairs. I wondered if there was still something going on in the main conference room after the welcome speeches. It wasn't that late.

I walked around the corner to the elevators and rode up to the fourth floor. It was quieter there. I did hear water from a shower come on in one of the rooms. Someone was home. Not everyone was a writer, though.

The door to room 491 was closed. I used my pass key to open it. Lyle might get angry with me for going inside without him, but I was acting on a hunch. The door creaked ever so slightly as I opened it slowly, my heart feeling as if it were in my throat.

The smell hit me. Metallic and something like dirty diaper. I covered my mouth and walked in. The smell hadn't been there earlier.

Melissa was on the bed, which was covered in messy sheets. Blood spilled from numerous small cuts all over. One foot hung over the edge of the bed and I noted the heel on her boot had broken off. I moved closer, though I didn't want to.

Just then, Melissa groaned. I rushed to the room phone to call Addy. She needed a doctor, now!

Chapter Sixteen

I stayed in the room, despite the smell, and looked around hoping to see if anything looked more out of place, but the whole room was a mess so I couldn't tell. The bathroom towels were scattered around the floor; I didn't trust that they were clean. Instead, I pulled at Melissa's sweater and added direct pressure to her wounds.

She moaned louder when I did that, her head moving back and forth, but her eyes didn't open. I wanted her to stay unconscious until I had someone there who could help.

Jake from security was the first one there, followed by Lyle. Lyle had rope and his park kit. Jake had the hotel's large first aid kit. Jake rounded the far side of the bed and climbed on, checking Melissa over. He pulled out a pen light to check her eyes and then put it away. I'd never been so glad that we required at least one person on the security team to have extensive emergency medical training, just in case.

I'd expected to have to have someone use the defibrillator not have someone deal with a stabbing victim, but fortunately, Jake's training extensive.

Lyle tossed off his coat and rope and opened his case, pulling out large pads for wounds. He held them out to Jake who pressed them over the wound areas.

"Make sure Addy has someone open the med center," Jake said.

I backed off, my hands bloody. "Already done," I said. I'd also asked if any of the guests had medical training.

Addy was searching through the information to see if anyone had added doctor to their prefix. If not, she'd call Nell and see if Nell knew of anyone who was a doctor. Melissa's wounds were going to need more work than Jake or Lyle's training could offer.

I stood back, wondering if it would be safe to wash my hands in the bathroom or if I needed to stand there.

"What prompted you to look in here?" Lyle asked.

"Addy thought of it. And then, I figured most of the writers had been asked about where Melissa was. She wouldn't be in one of their rooms and not be reported. If they tried killing her in a room, housekeeping would probably notice, at least at the end of the conference. Maybelle's keycard was missing so I figured it was the one place that someone could easily get to if they wanted privacy."

"Hall cameras," Jake said. "When I finish here, I'll have someone concentrate on this floor."

"End room," Lyle said. "It'd be easy enough to move the camera down here a hair to avoid notice at this door."

"Are you thinking that Melissa was the target and someone just wanted Maybelle's room?" I asked.

"I'm not really thinking anything just yet," Lyle said. "Hopefully, we can get Melissa stabilized enough that she can tell us who tried to kill her."

The two men worked over her for some time. I listened as they ripped clothing that hadn't already been torn. Watched as they applied more pressure bandages. Finally, a couple of workers brought up a gurney.

The two workers along with Lyle and Jake worked to bring Melissa over to the gurney and then they headed downstairs. I waited until they all left, then flipped off the lights and locked the door. I left faint traces of blood on the knob. I really needed to wash my hands, but first I needed to make sure we deactivated Maybelle's keycard, in order to make sure there were no other incursions into the room.

I crowded into the elevator with the others. When the company had remodeled the hotel, they'd expanded the employee elevator so we were easily able to fit the gurney and five people.

"Can you handle watching her until they find a doctor?" Jake asked Lyle. "I want to get to security and check footage for that hallway myself. We need to figure out who's doing this."

I'd have liked to know why as well, but I didn't say a word. No use bringing my own curiosity into the equation.

On the main level, I let the four of them head off towards the med center, which was down towards the back of the building. Most guests wouldn't ever need it and those who did probably only had a few scrapes or bruises. Now and again, someone twisted or sprained an ankle and we could either bandage it or call for an ambulance, depending on how they were doing overall and who they were with. After all, it was much different sending someone off to town with another person who was calm and able to drive versus someone who might be in the hotel on their own.

Twice we had heart attacks and once we had a stroke victim. In those cases, we had someone around who could get them stable enough for transport to the appropriate hospital facilities. In all cases, we'd had decent enough weather to do so.

I slipped into one of the public restrooms to wash my hands. Thankfully, no one was around as I let the blood swirl down the drain. A couple of women I recognized from around the hotel with writer lanyards came in just as I was wiping down the last of the red drops against the white porcelain.

One of the women, her hair in a long red braid, narrowed her eyes as she noticed that but when she saw me watch her expression, she hurriedly turned away and scurried into a stall. In a few minutes, in some circles, I'd now be a suspect.

Chapter Seventeen

Addy was still at the front desk when I returned. She appeared to be working on the computer, though there would be little to do. I didn't worry that she was playing a game. Even if Addy were the sort, we had no internet.

"I couldn't find anyone with a Dr. before their name or an MD after it," Addy said, looking up. "I called Nell's room but there's no answer. I don't know where she is or if there are any healthcare providers of any sort with the writers. Should I make an announcement?"

I sighed. The music from the bar was louder now, moving into later evening. Fewer people were sitting around in the reception area, but I heard voices that seemed to come up through the floor. The smell of pizza had taken over.

A brave or foolish person or someone really addicted was out under the portico, shivering while smoking a cigarette. That wasn't usually considered a smoking area but in this weather, I wasn't going to tell them to leave.

If we made an announcement asking for a doctor, people would wonder what was happening and we'd field questions from guests who wanted to know why we needed one. We'd also potentially get unqualified people who wanted to play the hero. If we didn't make an announcement, we might miss out on a guest who legitimately had some medical training.

"Tell you what," I said. "Call up to the forensic technicians' room. Let them know what happened and that they'll need to examine the room for Lyle, but also ask if either of them have more than basic medical training. It's a start."

Lyle hadn't asked me to call them, but I knew he'd want them to look at the room again. It would also give us a timeline of when they'd left the room originally which might help Jake narrow down how many hours of video he had to go through. At least now he had a specific area of the hotel and not the whole thing. And Lyle hadn't had to go out in the snow.

Addy picked up the phone. I drummed my fingers on the desk, then turned and went down to the med center.

Lyle had cut off most of Melissa's clothing. One of the security people was assisting. Wayne sat outside, dozing in a chair. He'd been on an early shift and probably needed the extra sleep. It wasn't likely that anyone would bother us here. He jumped when he noticed I was in the doorway.

"Sorry," he said.

I waved a hand at him. "You appear to be doing double duty."

"And I have a shift starting at two," he said, yawning.

Hopefully the snow would stop sooner than expected and we could get someone out here to help us.

"What?" Lyle yelled not looking at me. He grabbed a bottle of something and wetted a gauze square and started scrubbing an area around one of the wounds.

"No doctors that Addy can find. Nell's not in her

room," I said. "Addy is calling your techs to examine the room and to ask if either of them have medical training."

"I think Paul has might have had some in army," Lyle said. "But it's been a while. Better than nothing, I guess."

"I can make an announcement, but you know that's going to let everyone know we have someone injured."

Lyle sighed. "Let's wait on that. I'll have Paul make the call. This is definitely beyond the injuries I can handle, at least for more than a couple of hours."

I nodded, though Lyle couldn't possibly see me. The security person helping Lyle cut more strips of cloth and gently teased them away from bloodied areas around Melissa's arms. I turned away. I am not normally squeamish, but I also didn't normally have to look at guests all cut to shreds with some sort of knife.

I wondered if it was the same kind of filed knife that had been used to murder Maybelle. I'd call over to hospitality and make sure the kitchen workers knew to inventory the steak knives we set out for guests and to be sure they were all returned after being used. It was unusual to not get back all the silverware. Perhaps one of the servers had noticed something.

Walking back up to the desk, I had to admit to feeling a bit useless. I was a manager. I normally managed things. I ought to be on the phone finding a way to get someone here to help Melissa. I ought to be making sure the police had all the information they needed. I was doing what I could, helping Lyle with clues and making sure he had what he needed. And while I was trying to find someone who could help Melissa, it wasn't the same, not exactly.

The walk seemed to take forever, though I knew it was my imagination. My mind was racing but my limbs felt heavy and tired. I glanced at my phone, pleased that although there was no service, it at least told the time. After ten. So right around my normal bedtime.

Both my night manager, Addy, and my day manager, Mark, were at the desk now. Four of the writers and a couple of people without lanyards who may or may not have been writers were crowded around the desk.

Mark looked over at me like a drowning person seeking help.

"What's going on," I asked softly when he stepped back from his customer.

"They all want to know about Melissa," he said. "I have no idea how word got out, but it did. And I don't know a thing."

"I don't know much either." I stepped up to the desk anyway. As the Inn's manager, I needed to be the one to make the final decision on what was said.

"Can I help you?" I asked the man in front of me. I didn't recognize him. He didn't look like one of the writers. In fact, he looked like a skier.

"I heard that there's been several murders here and I want to know how long it's going to be before we can leave. I also think that you ought to comp our rooms for us seeing we aren't in the safe place you advertised," he said.

"We have had a single death," I replied as calmly as I could. Melissa was attacked, not dead, after all. "And while the police are investigating it, as they are required to do when a death is unattended, there have not been several deaths. Nor do I believe all my guests are at risk."

I crossed my fingers hoping the word "all" kept me from lying to the man. I thought all the writers were at risk, but not all the guests. He didn't seem like he was a writer. The white around his eyes and the tan on the lower part of his face suggested skier or snowboarder.

"Still, a hotel with a dead person? That's creepy. You should comp us something," he said.

"I advertise the Inn as being haunted," I said. "Do you really think no one died here before?"

He had no response to that. I was willing to comp him a couple of meals but I was going to make him work for it. I didn't want him to start telling all his friends, who were probably at the bar, that there was free food. Or worse, free rooms.

Instead of pressing, the man shrugged and walked off. He didn't look particularly happy, but I pushed that aside and looked at the next person.

She was clearly a writer. One of the younger ones considering her face had not a single line to speak of and her eyes made her look like a rather surprised cat. In fact, all of her was rather round, though she wasn't terribly wide.

"I'm Petra Ryne. I'm one of the writers," she said. "When I'm not writing cozies, I work as an ER nurse. I heard that someone was injured?" Her voice was low.

I avoided doing a jig, but only just. It didn't seem respectful.

"Come with me," I said, leading her around the side of the desk. I couldn't help but notice that everyone crowded around us was watching.

Petra followed me quickly and purposefully. She seemed like the kind of nurse who exuded confidence.

Once we were on our way down the hallway, I asked her how she knew we had an injury.

"Everyone is talking," she said. "I think someone saw a gurney being moved from the med center. I didn't notice that you advertised a doctor on duty, so I figured you just had a basic infirmary where someone would rest until help came."

"That's about our set-up. I have a couple of people with advanced first aid training but no real medical training that I know of," I said.

"I'm not a doctor," Petra said quietly, "So don't expect too much."

"We don't have a lot to work with, either," I said. "We're not that isolated so it's mostly a matter of helping someone stabilize if they have a wound or a heart attack. We are definitely not set up for this."

We reached the medical center. The walk was faster with company. I noticed one of the forensic techs was in there.

"Is she a doctor?" the security guard asked, looking up. The two men were still cleaning the cuts.

"ER nurse," Petra said. "Let me see what you've got and what kinds of things you have access to."

"There are plenty of cuts, but only a few of them are deep," Paul said. "Most have pressure bandages that were put on at the scene. We're cleaning up around the main wounds and I'm just starting to pull off the pressure bandages to see what's underneath. If you have sewing skills, that would be great. Not something I've done in a long time and a few of these appear to need sutures."

Petra moved into the crowd around the gurney. My security person stepped back, looking a little uncomfortable.

"Do I need to be here now?" she whispered to me. "Wayne took off to get some sleep and I thought seeing it was just Melissa and Lyle I ought to stay and then Paul arrived and it still felt weird to leave her alone with two men but now…"

"Go on and get back to your regular duties," I said.

Lyle's radio, one of our security radios came on with static.

"Lyle, please come to the security office," Jake announced.

"On my way," Lyle said. "Over."

The radio just clicked off. While he had to wash up before he could leave, I didn't need to wait. I headed to security to see what Jake had found. Hopefully a nice close-up of whoever went into Maybelle's room with Melissa.

The security office was downstairs, so on my way there, I passed the main conference room and noticed the doors were closed. I tested the latch and found it open. I poked my head inside, only to find several of my housekeeping people working. One vacuumed while another set the chairs up again. The room smelled faintly of coffee and the various teas that were served. The long table in the back was empty, but new pots of coffee and hot water would be out in the morning.

I backed out, wondering where Nell was and if I should go back and try and call her again. The life of a conference organizer was busy on conference days, though, so it was unlikely she'd made it back to her room.

The sound of the vacuum cut off when the door closed behind me, leaving only the sounds of the basement. I wasn't surprised to get a chill as I walked down the dogleg that ended in the employee only area. I glanced back to see Clara running, staring behind her in a silent scream.

With all the activity, her ghost was certainly getting active. I hoped that some of the ghost hunters in the group got to see her. I wondered about Frank who wanted to stay in the supposedly haunted suite. I hadn't seen him down in the basement, but perhaps a dead maid wasn't nearly as interesting as ABC Smithers.

I pushed through the door labelled "employees only" and went down the back staircase to the sub-basement. I could have taken the employee elevator directly to the sub-basement, but I had wanted to see who might be hanging around by the conference room. They might have had something to tell me.

The security office was just to the left of the stairwell. The office was actually a warren of several rooms, only one of which contained the monitors of the hotel hallways and public areas.

"What did you find?" I asked Jake, who was sitting in his private office. It wasn't even as large as mine, but he had a computer with several monitors where he could check things from time to time just to make sure his people were doing what they were supposed to be.

"We've reviewed four hours of footage from when Melissa disappeared. She goes into the room alone, using a keycard. Something we didn't find on her when we were there," Jake said.

"Was someone there before her?" I asked. It didn't seem likely that another person could have wedged the door open without someone noticing.

"No one goes in or out for that time," Jake said. "At least not on tape. Several guests walk around, but there are enough differences that no one patched the tape with a long rewind. It's possible they covered just a short time frame, but Brandon, our main computer wiz who'd be able to say for certain, isn't here."

Brandon was not one of the security people who had

stayed. His father was elderly and suffered from dementia. It wasn't so bad that his dad couldn't live on his own, but now and then he'd wander out and forget why he was out. It had happened only once in the last year, but it was enough that if the weather was at all bad, Brandon chose to stay with him.

I had no doubt he'd been there bright and early this morning making sure that his father had everything he might need. In fact, I wouldn't be surprised to find out he was sleeping on the sofa by the front door, just to make sure his dad didn't decide to go for an evening walk in the storm.

"The police will have people who can do that, too," I said. I sighed. I had hoped we'd have an answer.

"This was planned," Jake said. "I don't know if Melissa was part of it, seeing she had a key, or if someone lured her there."

Lyle pushed his way in. "What've you got?"

"Just that Melissa let herself in with the key. I see no one coming in after or before, for several hours. I watched until I saw Maggie enter the room," Jake said. "I think the footage may have been doctored."

"Can you find out how it might have been done or pick up anything from before?" Lyle asked.

"Brandon might be able to," Jake said, "But he's not on duty."

Lyle sighed, sounding not unlike I had just a moment ago.

"We'll have to wait until the weather clears and the police can take a look," I said quietly.

Lyle shook his head. "We've got one dead person and one injured. I don't know how long we can wait."

"I'm going to try calling Nell again. I noticed she wasn't in the main conference room so perhaps she's in her room. She might know if someone in the group is a doctor," I said.

"I asked Petra but she didn't know anyone," Lyle said. He stared at the video morosely. I hated it when he got into moods where he was grumpy and pessimistic.

"Still…" I said, turning to go.

"How long could a door remain open with a jam before someone would notice?" Lyle asked before I got to out of the room.

I turned back, wondering what Jake would say.

"If it was tape to keep the latch from engaging, probably until the next person came in," he said. "The door would open too easily and you wouldn't feel the latch turning. They'd notice."

"I made sure the door was latched when we left after looking through it," I said. "I'm sure that your forensics people would have done the same." At least I hoped they would.

Lyle nodded.

"Someone would have had to have been watching," Jake said. "Because it's only a few hours between when the techs leave and when Melissa enters."

"I need to ask Kendra if she knows where her sister got that key," Lyle said.

"I'm going to look at who's in the rooms closest to this one. If it's another writer, maybe it's the killer," I said.

Lyle shrugged. At an earlier point during the day, he would have shown some enthusiasm. He hated not having an answer. In the parks, he could keep looking around and find some clue to what was going on. He understood the outdoors. He was good with people and could handle light investigations, but I knew this would haunt him for years, whether or not we found the person who was doing this.

I took the back elevator up. I took a slight detour to the

medical center and glanced in. Petra was still there with the forensic tech, Paul.

"I wish I had an antibiotic," Petra said, clipping a bit of thread. She didn't see me watching.

I left without a word. I wished we had a more well-stocked medical center, too. Maybe I'd put in a word with the owners after this about keeping a doctor on staff at least part-time or having someone on call who could stay at the hotel during bad weather.

Up front, I glanced around the reception area. It hadn't changed much since earlier, but the music seemed even louder, or maybe I'd just been pleasantly insulated in other parts of the Inn and wasn't used to it.

Addy was alone again. I went into my office, taking a moment to savor the smell of wood and coffee, things that made the room mine. I rubbed my hands against the smooth grain of the desk and then got to work looking up the guests on that end of the fourth floor. Two of them were writers.

Diana McPherson and Laura Wells. I jotted a note to look into both of them and left it for Lyle. They might have something to do with the attack or maybe they heard something. Weren't mystery writers supposed to be observant?

I yawned. It was time for me to go back and try and get some sleep, though I had a feeling that wasn't happening easily, not that night.

"I've been over at the restaurant most of the evening and not once has Smithers appeared," Frank was complaining to Addy when I left the office.

"I'm very sorry you haven't seen him, but he doesn't keep a schedule and it's not like we can tell him you're waiting for him," Addy explained with more patience than I felt.

"I'm beginning to think this is all a scam," Frank snapped.

I slipped back into my office, not wanting to deal with him. Addy was more awake and had more ability to act patient than I did right at that moment.

I heard Frank continue to complain for a few more minutes. Addy's voice never changed. She really was quite impressive. Normally, I was off when she was on duty. A few years ago, I'd observed her work at the front desk. When the night manager position had come open and she'd applied, I'd worried that she wouldn't be up to it, but she'd learned the lessons she needed to learn and now I trusted that the Inn was in good hands when she was on duty. Never more so than now.

Finally, slapping his hand against the desk, Frank left. I counted to thirty before I heard a sigh and Addy turned to come into the office and flopped into the chair.

"I'm not sure what's up with him," she said. "Last night he complained about Smithers as well. I suggested he go down to the lower level and wait to see Clara. She's been around several times. I heard a quick scream and then giggles at about two in the morning yesterday, and then someone came up and told me they'd seen a ghost."

"I've seen her several times. I heard there was another sighting of Smithers in the restaurant, though." I leaned back.

"And Frank heard as well. He was not pleased. It's almost as if he thinks he set up a special appointment with the ghosts. He also wants to know more about the ghost in his suite, but I don't know anything about that." Addy made a face.

"Neither do I. I suspect that someone staying here made up a story about seeing a ghost when they really didn't. Probably one of the horror authors who stayed here when I offered free rooms," I said. "They wanted to get their money's worth."

Addy laughed. "Well, I wish they'd given us a few details so we could fill them in for Frank. Even if the ghost was made up, he can't get any angrier than he already is."

"I should go back and try and get some sleep," I said, closing out the computer. "Or try."

"And I should run the check-out report and bills," Addy said. "Not that I think anyone is checking out tomorrow. Even if they planned to, I don't think they'll be able to."

"Maybe by afternoon?" I said hopefully.

"Snow isn't even supposed to stop until mid-morning," Addy said. "Although maybe it will be light enough that they can start plowing the road."

I wasn't hopeful. The highways would get treated first, although I suspect the plows had been running along them for some time. After the main highways, would be the secondary main roads and those through town. Local streets to town would be next on the list and finally, the road to our turnoff would be remembered. It was nice to be so secluded, except when storms hit.

With any luck, though, the cell tower just had interference, perhaps some ice, and when that melted, we'd have service again.

The lights flickered for a minute, but didn't go out as they had earlier in the day. I'd have been surprised, considering we were on generator power and those were well maintained. I knew we had plenty of fuel. Even so, the computers reset themselves and Addy had to log back in.

I left her to it and walked down the stairs to my apartment. I was more awake now than I had been earlier and I didn't hold out much hope for getting any sleep. I didn't see anyone around but a lone housekeeper vacuuming the main area. She looked up and said hello.

As I entered the employee area, I heard whispers from in the dorms. But it sounded like most people were trying to be considerate of their fellow dorm-mates. I hoped I'd have workers who were awake in the morning. If the snow stopped, we'd be getting a lot of questions about checking out and the condition of the roads. Hopefully, we'd have real power and cell service, if not internet, again.

I'd left the lights on in the living room in my apartment. Latte and Chai were on the bed when I went in to change clothing. Chai let me know he was not pleased with this disruption to his routine. I could heartily say I agreed with him.

Chapter Nineteen

Given how hard it was to wake myself up the next morning, I must have slept, though my body didn't feel refreshed. I didn't remember dreams, but I did remember tossing and turning. Chai was on the chair in the corner of my bedroom, looking annoyed. Latte appeared from the living room. I must have been tossing a lot to annoy both cats so much they left the queen-sized bed.

"Sorry guys," I said, yawning. Hopefully, a shower would wake me up and then some coffee that I'd make down here. I'd grab some from the café for later. It was definitely going to be a multi-cup day.

My morning routine finished, the bitter taste of black coffee perking up a few more brain cells, and I was ready for a normal day. The view out the window of the piles of snow and the flurries still coming down, though more lightly, didn't bode well for a normal day. I had, I hoped, a wounded woman in the med center. If she'd died, someone would have called, at least I thought so.

I ate a piece of toast I barely tasted, while I stood in front of my window and tried to mentally make a list of all the things that needed doing. There might not be any room changeovers thanks to the weather, but there would be those who had hoped to check-out today and others who would be calling to cancel because they couldn't check in. I had to go over the inventory and get a sense of how much food we were going through each day. While there were rough estimates, I liked to know exactly how much my guests were eating and what things we were likely to run out of. The chefs kept up on that and did specials on items not selling as well, but as the manager, I wanted to keep my hand in.

I'd make sure that spa services, off in the new wing on the first floor, had everything they needed. The writers were no doubt keeping themselves busy. In fact, they had an early breakfast today and would be using the small conference rooms. Hopefully, they'd do so without any more surprises.

I took a deep breath, finished my coffee and headed down the hallway. A quick bump from behind me in the dorms startled me, making me jump, just as Olive appeared.

"I see you have someone in the med center," Olive said.

"She was stabbed or cut multiple times in Maybelle's room," I said. "I don't suppose you noticed anything."

Olive made a face as if I were asking a foolish question.

"Yes, I saw someone nearly murdered in the Inn and just didn't think it important enough to share," she said, rolling her eyes.

Okay. Yeah. Foolish. Olive hated anything going wrong at the inn as much as I did. In fact, probably more so. She'd been attached to the place for more years than I was even before she'd died.

"See anything that might be suspicious? It looked like someone was in the room before Melissa got there," I said.

"Is that the woman you were looking for? With the sister?" Olive asked.

I nodded.

"Interesting. The sister was alone last evening, but she picked up the phone twice and held it to her ear as if talking, about three times. She didn't push any buttons so I would guess she got calls," Olive said. "I did think it strange that she wasn't with her sister. They seemed to be rather connected and I wanted to keep an eye on them as they were some of the last to see Maybelle, or so you said."

"And now one of them has been injured, possibly left for dead," I said. "It was just luck that when Kendra couldn't find her sister, I decided to look in Maybelle's room."

"So you think someone wanted her dead?" Olive asked.

"I do. I'm worried that whoever it was might have used another one of our steak knives sharpened to a point. I've made a note to hospitality to be sure we get all steak knives back."

"Our knives were never particularly unique, though," Olive said. "It's not impossible they brought their own. It wouldn't even be difficult if they were driving. All they needed was a single trip up to the restaurant here at another time and they'd be set."

Unfortunately, Olive was right. I walked up the stairs and smiled at an author hurrying down, walking around Olive without noticing that she didn't exactly step up on the stairs but just floated up, though her feet moved. If I watched, it bothered me. She looked like someone had done a bad job of editing two different video tapes together.

"You're right," I said when the author was far enough past. Reaching the first floor, I noted a group waiting by the elevator. A few people milled about the main reception area but none of them wore the lanyards the authors had.

Olive followed me to the main desk, but disappeared as I opened the door. I heard a gasp from someone by the elevator, so at least one of them noticed that Olive hadn't walked through the door.

Suzanne was at the desk. I went into my office and pulled up the computer notes. Addy had two people scheduled to check out this morning and she'd given them their receipts and made notes to ask them if they really wanted to check out or remain for another day. Suzanne had a note that one of the guests had already called and asked to stay another night.

I had no problem with that considering I couldn't imagine someone driving to the hotel in this weather. Unfortunately, with our internet down I had no idea how many cancellations we had. Most of them had already come in before the storm started so I wasn't particularly worried about a stranded traveler. I'd find them a place somewhere. There were a couple of rooms left, though they were the ones closest to the ice machines, which tended to be a bit noisy.

Lyle had left no notes. I sighed. I needed more coffee.

"I'm getting a cup of coffee from the café. You want one?" I asked Suzanne.

She shook her head. "I'm good for now. I've had a bunch of people asking when the storm is supposed to end."

"Addy said she heard late morning, but it will probably be at least a day before we're plowed out and that's likely only after we get through to the emergency services about our injured guest." Injured was a nice way of putting it.

Suzanne nodded. "I think one of the techs asked to use our phone when I came on. Tall guy. Blonde? Named Paul?"

I nodded. I hoped he hadn't stayed up all night with Melissa. We had security to spell him if needed.

"He was able to get through on a call out to emergency services about the third try," Suzanne said. "Before that he kept getting a busy signal, which he said he shouldn't have gotten."

I remembered the old days when busy signals just told you that all circuits were busy. It was possible part of the landline system was down as well or not working as well as it should. I didn't bother to explain that to Suzanne.

"Did he say when they thought they could get here?" I asked.

"They'll make it a priority. And we're to plow as much as we can. Even if they can't drive in here, they're hoping to get a helicopter in as soon as the wind dies down and the snow clears a bit more."

"Is someone on that?" I asked.

"I talked to Wayne in security and he contacted someone in maintenance. They've already started but it's slow going with of all the cars in the lot," Suzanne said.

I gave her a nod, glad that we would soon be out of this mess and the authorities could take over. I headed out to get coffee and then check on Melissa.

The café was less crowded than the day before. Of course, the writers had their own conference breakfast. I grabbed a cup and nodded at the waitress. Normally she worked a later shift but she must have volunteered to stay on.

Then, I hurried back down the hall towards the med center. The hot bitter taste of the brew felt like the only thing keeping me moving. Petra dozed in the chair next to Melissa, her eyes snapping open when I came in.

"Did you get any sleep?" I asked.

Petra yawned. "Not really. She had a few incidents of gasping for air and I worried we were going to lose her. There wasn't anything to tell me if we were dealing with heart or lungs or what. Paul finally took off to get some sleep. I'm hoping someone can spell me later. Long shifts in the ER mean I'm not unfamiliar with this kind of schedule, but I was hoping this would be a bit of a vacation."

"I'm surprised you find time to write," I said.

Petra smiled. "Writing is what I do for relaxation. My main character is a nurse in assisted living and she's always getting involved in little mysteries around her charges."

"It sounds like you put your nursing knowledge to good use even when you relax," I said.

That elicited a shrug. Petra got up to check on Melissa. She was breathing, which was about all I could tell.

"Suzanne tells me that Paul called out and got ahold of emergency services," I said.

"Did he?" Petra said. "He left about two and didn't tell me."

I frowned. Suzanne didn't come on that early. It seemed weird that Paul would come down and use the phone later in the morning. Maybe he'd just realized it and decided to try the main desk phone rather than the room phone.

"I should go double check," I said. "In case it was someone else. Will someone be relieving you soon?"

"I think Jake, the head of security, said he'd be in around nine," Petra said. "She's been reasonably stable right now. Did you ever find Nell to ask if there were any doctors in the group?"

I shook my head. "I have to admit to giving up and going to bed."

"I don't blame you. It was a long day." Petra checked Melissa's vitals and then settled back in her chair. I went back to the desk, still frowning, wondering who had called from the desk.

Suzanne was in the back when I got there. No one else was around.

"Are you sure the person who called was Paul?" I asked.

"I think that's what he told me, why?"

"Petra said Paul left about two this morning to go up to bed."

"That's hours before I was even on. Do you suppose he couldn't sleep?" Suzanne's eyes were wide.

"It seems like someone in his field should be able to sleep when they need to." I didn't like it. I tried calling out on the main phone line and didn't get a busy signal. I got the funky tone that says there is no dial tone.

"I'm not getting anything. I'll let Lyle know and perhaps he can get through on the radio. Or maybe the real Paul can get through on their radio," I said.

I hated the fact that I now felt tied to the desk, but I didn't want Suzanne alone. There was a good chance she'd encountered the killer or perhaps an associate of the killer. That might put her in danger if there was any possibility she knew he wasn't the real forensic technician.

Lyle had no doubt been up even longer than I had been. I hated to call him. I wished there were a way to text that wasn't through a cell phone so I could just drop him a note. Well, when he got there, I'd be at the front desk, helping Suzanne whether she needed it or not. At the very least, I'd stay nearby in the reception area.

The next hour passed slowly. The writers made up

many of our guests and they were all downstairs. I heard faint clapping multiple times and each time, I braced for a deluge of people coming up the stairs and the elevator, but nothing. Other guests walked through the reception area to the elevators with barely a look at us.

A few people gathered by the front doors, looking out. The big window was still ice covered and impossible to see through. I hoped that the snow hadn't started up harder. I did hear the growling sounds of our plow and the beeping when the driver backed up. It was certainly possible those fascinated by the goings on outside were worried about their cars.

Lyle showed up about the time I was ready to go get a refill on my coffee. I had just finished telling myself that Suzanne could hold off an assailant for the few minutes I'd be gone.

"I need to talk to you," I said. "In my office."

Lyle sighed, his eyes bloodshot and his hair still wet from a quick shower.

"What?" he asked, moving around the desk to take my chair.

"A blonde man asked Suzanne if he could use the desk phone and call emergency response. He intimated that he was one of the forensic techs."

"Probably Paul. So what?" Lyle asked. He ran a hand through his hair and then eyed my mug longingly.

"Petra said Paul left the med center at around two. Suzanne doesn't get in until around five. Either Paul came back down to make that call or someone impersonated him," I said.

That made Lyle sit up and nod.

"I'll go get you a cup of coffee while you noodle that," I said. "But I'm rather worried about Suzanne alone at the desk. Mark will be down later on to help out and I'll let him know that she's not to be left alone as well."

Lyle sighed. "Thanks."

"I also left you the names of the two writers whose rooms are closest to Maybelle's. It's probably a breach of privacy or something, but lives are more important than privacy, at least I think so."

Lyle grunted at me and I left to head back to the café, thankful that Suzanne wasn't completely alone at the desk, although Lyle was sleepy enough that he might as well be useless.

I hurried to the cafe and noticed Frank, our intrepid ghost hunter hunched over a large paper in a corner. At the same table, sitting next to him, was a broader blonde man I hadn't seen before. As he raised his eyes over a cup of coffee to watch me grab another mug, I nodded and smiled, hoping I didn't turn away too quickly or appear to be staring too hard.

Frank had registered as a single. I began to wonder if he'd lied about that. Or perhaps this was just a friend he knew staying in another room. All the same, the look of the man made my hands shake slightly as I carried coffee back to Lyle and tell him what I'd seen.

Chapter Twenty

I watched as Lyle strode over to the café to get a look at the person with Frank. Maybe even to interview the two of them, just because they were staying at the hotel. I started to follow but he glared at me, so I stayed with Suzanne.

"I wish he'd let you go and maybe let him know if that was the man you saw at the desk," I said.

"But then he'd know I knew he wasn't the technician," Suzanne said. She'd finally put together that knowing that it hadn't been the tech who had called put her in danger.

I tried the phone again. This time I got a dial tone. I tried 911 but nothing went through. I hung up and got the funky ring sound that signaled there was no connection. Definitely still having problems.

"I'm going to see how our plows are doing," I said. If the regular plows got to the entrance to our road the inn's plows would get the private road we were on, at least enough to get an emergency vehicle through. It might not have stopped snowing, but better to start now than to do nothing.

Suzanne didn't look happy about being left alone, even

if I was just going to be across the room. Just as I left the confines of the desk area, Kendra came out of the elevator. She was dressed in jeans and a long-sleeved t-shirt with embroidered flowers. Her gray hair was trimmed to her shoulders and it swung as she walked, though she didn't make eye contact with me. That would make sense if she were shy.

As she approached the desk, I slipped through the door into my office behind the desk and listened.

"I'm wondering about my sister, Melissa," Kendra said. Her voice was low but surprisingly harsh.

"She's in the med center," Suzanne said. "You can go visit her if you want."

Kendra shook her head. "I don't want. I just want to know how she is."

I noted that she made eye-contact with Suzanne without a problem. I walked out to the front and stood next to Suzanne.

Kendra noticed me and held my gaze. This wasn't exactly what I expected of someone considered social awkward and shy.

"She was sleeping last I checked," I said. "The nurse with her was concerned about her last night, but she seems to have stabilized. We're trying to contact emergency services to make sure someone can get out here as soon as possible."

"What did the doctor say?" Kendra asked.

I frowned. I had told Addy to call up to Kendra's room. It hadn't occurred to me that she didn't go down all night and knew almost nothing.

"We don't have a doctor on staff," I said. "One of the forensic technicians used to be a medic in the army and we have an ER nurse with her. Our detective and our head of security have extensive first aid training to assist."

"How can you be so isolated and not have a doctor?" Kendra asked. Again, her gaze was direct and possibly even a bit harsher than before.

"We've never had an issue prior to this," I said. "We normally only need the med center for basic first aid or for an area to isolate someone until the first responders arrive."

Shaking her head, Kendra reminded me a bit of Frank. "I can't believe you don't even have a doctor. You'd think with all the warning about the storm that you'd have had time to contact someone and have them come in."

"As I said, this is a first. Normally, we don't have people with such extensive injuries."

Kendra sniffed. "I'm missing the writer's conference thanks to this."

As if that was the most important thing.

"I'm sorry about that. I'm sure if you talk to Nell…"

Kendra was already shaking her head. "I have no desire to talk to Nell. Or anyone else associated with that conference. I wanted to listen, not be spoken down to because I'm older than most of the other writers."

I wanted to ask about her other friends, but I bit my tongue. Maybe they were Melissa's friends. Whoever had said Kendra was shy, was completely wrong. She wasn't socially adept, certainly. I thought of all the neurodivergent labels I'd heard of and wondered if she fit into one of those categories more than just shy. Or perhaps fear made her act aggressively. She was not what I had expected.

She left as abruptly as she arrived, not heading to the café or to the stairs, but heading to the elevator. I took a moment to glance back as I went back to the door and saw it was going up.

Suzanne gave me a hopeful look upon catching my eye, but I just waved and walked across the reception area. A few people were standing there. Our bellhop was a girl this morning, though I didn't recognize her and her back remained to me so I didn't see a name tag. I tried to know all the employees, but it was hard at an inn this size, especially because I didn't often work the night shift and probably half the people volunteering to stay had been late night workers.

I looked out over the tops of heads and saw our plow working back and forth on the edge of the driveway. I saw plenty of flakes still coming down, too. Not as hard as they had earlier, but definitely not appearing as if they'd be stopping any time soon. We really needed the weather to clear up.

If emergency services didn't know we needed help, it was unlikely that we would be getting a helicopter in here. Even so, I wasn't going to stop our people from plowing what they could and then doing the road. Once we did get a message out, someone could get here sooner.

I went back to the desk. Suzanne's shoulders lowered and her eyes radiated relief. She was really worried.

"The plow is working but it's definitely still snowing," I said.

We both looked at the clock. It wasn't quite what anyone could call midmorning but obviously we both wanted it to be.

Lyle came back followed first by Frank and then by the blonde man. I said nothing to Suzanne as they approached. Lyle brought Frank into the office first. The blonde man stared at Suzanne and me. I gave a tight-lipped smile of the sort I hoped I'd give to anyone waiting to be questioned.

He turned and paced around, hopefully out of earshot.

"Him?" I whispered to Suzanne as low as I could, keeping my eyes on him.

She gave the slightest nod.

Interesting. He wasn't wearing a lanyard so I didn't think he was one of the writers. He shouldn't have known Melissa or Maybelle and yet he appeared to have something to do with this. But what, I had no idea.

And Frank. He'd come to experience the ghosts. It was why he kept complaining about Smithers. And not seeing the ghost that we knew nothing about in room 785.

The desk phone rang. I reached out to answer without thinking. Suzanne's hand hovered over mine as I picked up the receiver.

"Front desk. Maggie speaking," I said.

"This is Paul Tillman, one of the techs. We got through to base on the radio, finally. They'll be prioritizing getting out here," he said. There was relief in his voice.

"Good news," I said. I had been more excited the first time I heard it, even if that time had turned out to be a lie.

"We also re-processed the hotel room," he said. "Tell Lyle, nothing new but a bunch of blood. We got some hairs but based on the length and color, I'd bet they belong to the vic."

"She has a sister with hair the same color," I said. "Maybe a bit longer, though."

"We'll keep that in mind," Paul said. "We're packing up to get ready to leave, even if it will be a few more hours."

"Thank you so much for all you've done," I said with feeling. Having another person who knew first aid had been a godsend at time when it was much needed. Paul had to be feeling the strain just like Petra.

I hung up the phone. Suzanne was watching the blonde man. She swallowed hard. I looked over at him, giving him my most intense stare. He held my gaze, a slight smile playing on his lips. I would report that to Lyle. I couldn't imagine what he was playing at. He had to know something or have done something.

Frank banged open the door of my office so hard I jumped. I was still watching the blonde man and he smirked as I did so.

I'm sure I glared even harder at him, though it wasn't at all productive.

"I'm here to find ghosts!" Frank practically yelled. "And you're ruining my vacation!"

I heard Lyle apologize for the inconvenience, but Frank was already throwing open the door to the reception area. The blonde man, still smirking, headed towards the door, almost as if he were waiting to talk to Lyle. If he were guilty of something, you'd think that he wouldn't be so eager to talk to the police.

Frank glared at Suzanne and me. For a moment I thought he was going to leave, but then he marched towards the desk, his face slightly red. It was the most color he'd had in his face the entire time.

"I'll be talking to my attorney about this," he said. "You're purposely harassing me! Probably because I'm going to tell everyone your hauntings are fake!"

A woman carrying a coffee was walking towards the elevators. I saw her glance over at him and give a slight eye roll. I almost laughed.

"We make no guarantees that anyone sees a ghost," I said. "We merely report when people do see them."

"You make it sound as if this place is haunted and that everyone will see ghosts!" Frank was now roaring loud enough that Suzanne stepped back a pace.

A couple of writers climbed the stairs from the basement and waited on the top one, watching.

"I'm sure our attorneys will be happy to talk with yours. Shall I get you their information?" I asked quietly.

"He should come down here," one of the women on the top step said.

The other laughed. "I kept getting the chills walking down that hallway and then seeing that woman…"

I didn't hear the rest.

Frank whirled, glaring at them.

Ghosts seemed attracted to unsettled energy. I was actually surprised that they weren't swarming around Frank.

"Give him a break," Olive said, appearing next to me. Frank had turned his back but he whirled around at the sound of a new voice.

"Oh it's you," he snapped. "You keep telling me to go places but I've never seen a ghost."

"Probably because ghosts don't like your energy," Olive said reasonably.

"Who is this woman?!" Frank was again in angry bull mode.

"This is Olive. She used to be the inn manager," I said.

"I can see why she was let go." Frank snapped.

"She wasn't," I replied calmly. "She died on the job."

And Olive, to her credit, slowly faded out just like that.

Frank backed up. "That's some sort of prank. That's not how ghosts look! I've seen ghosts." He pointed his finger at me. "I'll sue!"

I watched as he headed over towards the elevators. I looked at Suzanne and shrugged.

She shook her head.

"Honestly, I've never seen Olive before."

"We talk," I said, grinning. I wasn't willing to share that I thought of the ghost as my best friend. I was the boss. I didn't want staff thinking I was lonely or anything. I admit, that in personal life it's difficult for me to reach out and trust. Olive sort of popped in now and then, though she was very good about not popping in when I was indisposed. I remembered what she'd said about being able to see a bit when she wasn't visible and I shuddered. Maybe she watched and avoided surprising me when I was in the shower out of good manners. That didn't mean she didn't see me.

I pushed that thought away. It didn't bear thinking about. But really, Olive had been the one to reach out. Most of my friends were people who had reached out. Unfortunately, the hierarchy, such as it was, at the Inn, meant that the people I saw the most didn't feel comfortable reaching out to me and me asking them for a meal just wasn't my way.

Thinking back on this, I suppose I lasted as long as I did in this isolated place thanks to Olive and her friendship. I'd have to thank her the next time I saw her and we weren't caught up in this mystery.

Suzanne stared at me for a moment and then shrugged. "I didn't know any of our ghosts talked."

"Most don't," I said. "I'm not sure why Olive is different."

"They all have their quirks." Suzanne looked down at the system and typed something in.

I looked longingly at my office. I had reports to go over but Lyle was busy interviewing people, still. I ought to find a room downstairs and make him use that as a sort of base and not my office. I could work from my apartment, but I hated leaving Suzanne alone. Mark wouldn't be on for another half an hour. I sipped my coffee, hoping it would bring me answers to my questions. Maybe if I drank enough it would even make the snow stop.

Chapter Twenty-One

Lyle spent nearly an hour in the office with the blonde man I didn't know. When the door opened the man came out, still smirking. He didn't even glance at Suzanne. The smirk seemed reserved for me.

Right around that time, the bar started up some low music to welcome people in for an early lunch. Mark ought to be arriving at the desk any time.

Lyle followed the blonde man out and waited for him to exit the desk area. We both watched him head towards the elevators and press the up button. With all the writers downstairs, the elevator dinged quickly and the man disappeared.

"And?" I whispered to Lyle once the man was safely inside, riding up to his room.

"His name *is* Paul," Lyle said. "He did used to be a medical technician but in Ohio, not here. He's on vacation. He knows Frank because they're both ghost hunters. Basically, he tried to call out for emergency services. He thinks he did, finally. Nothing he said he was a lie, but it was clear from his attitude that he knew Suzanne would think he was someone else."

"Weird," I said.

"There are people like that—the ones who want to make a mess of things, particularly investigations," Lyle said quietly.

I nodded, making a face.

I heard noises from downstairs. Several people walked quickly up the stairs. Lyle disappeared again, into my office, without even asking. I sighed.

A pair of women, dressed in boots, jeans, and sweaters, carrying jackets, hurried over to us. "Is the restaurant open?"

"It opens at 11:30."

"Even on a day like today?"

"Even on a day like today. Stay under the covered walkway and you should be good, so long as you have coats," I said, smiling.

"Great." I noticed they both had their hair in a single braid as they turned. One was long and brown. The other, shorter and pale blonde. I took a moment to reflect how often pals seemed to start looking like each other. I hoped I didn't start wearing twinsets to look like Olive. They were so last century.

The two went around the people looking out the window and headed outside. A few other women noticed them going out and followed. A couple of them were less than dressed for the weather. I hoped they didn't get frostbite.

An elderly man walked up to the desk, looking around at all the writers as they made their way to the restaurant or café. The conference had a special dinner that evening but attendees had to get their own lunch.

"So what's going on here?" he asked. He leaned his

small, bent frame against a rather ornately carved cane. His gray hair stuck out of his head in wisps.

"It's a writer's conference," I said, giving the easy answer. If he wasn't asking about the murder or the attack, I wasn't going to tell him. "I think they've just had a break for lunch."

"Must have a strong stomach to be here during this storm."

"Well, then you must, too." I gave him my best smile. He seemed nice enough. I wanted to ask what brought him to the inn but figured that whoever had checked him in had already done so and I hated to repeat questions.

"My wife loves this spa," he said. "She hasn't seen a ghost, but I swear we were at the restaurant once and saw Smithers. It's why I told Frank about this place. He's so into ghosts and monsters and such. He writes horror fiction, or wants to, anyway."

"You know the gentleman up in the suite that's supposed to be haunted?" I tried to smile again but hoped that I wasn't gritting my teeth. This man seemed so nice and kindly and Frank was something other.

"You're probably the only person to call Frank a gentleman," the old man laughed. "He used to be a nice guy. Then his ex started writing and selling books and he never got anywhere. It drove him nuts."

"Did she also write horror?" I asked.

"Oh no. She wrote mysteries. You know, like Agatha Christie type stuff. My wife loves them, which I always say is being disloyal to Frank, but she doesn't care. She never cared for him, much."

The old man picked his way back across the reception area towards the spa. I kept smiling at him, though my mind was racing. Frank had been married to a mystery writer, and if the old man was right, not just a mystery writer, but a cozy mystery writer. Which meant his ex could be here.

Frank might know more than he was saying and a disgruntled ex might be willing to spill beans on people he had cause to dislike. I needed to tell Lyle.

Chapter Twenty-Two

The smells of lunch filled the reception area, along with the smell of too many bodies crowding into one place. Plenty of writers were hanging out by the door, probably debating about going outside, but smart enough to know that they weren't necessarily dressed for the weather. A few of the people watching the plows moved away to find a better vantage point, though I doubted there was one. Most of the windows were covered in ice.

I tapped on my office door and waited for Lyle to say come in. It went on long enough that I started to fidget. I imagined Lyle lying there with blood leaking from a wound that he got having fallen or perhaps that Paul had inflicted earlier and Lyle was too proud to say anything about. I knew my imagination was running wild, but it was difficult to keep it under control.

Knocking again, this time louder, I leaned against the wood. Not that I could hear anything. The wood was old and therefore, thick.

"Come in!" Lyle snarled. Whatever he was working on had made him cranky.

"What?" he demanded when I entered.

"Did Frank mention his ex was a cozy mystery writer?" I asked.

Lyle's eyes widened and he leaned back in his chair. "No. In fact, he said he found all the writers rather distracting to his ghost hunting. He talked about writing horror novels and also a few non-fiction books on haunted places around the United States."

I nodded. "There's an elderly couple here who know him at least slightly. I guess the ex was more successful than Frank and he got very bitter about the whole thing. I was wondering if he mentioned it so you could ask him who his ex was."

"You're thinking it was Maybelle." Lyle made it a statement, not a question.

"It would explain some things."

"Not about Melissa, though." Lyle made a face.

"No, not about Melissa, unless she saw something she wasn't supposed to. Or maybe he was married to Melissa and Maybelle saw him planning something and said she'd warn her?" I suggested.

Lyle narrowed his eyes. "I like the first theory better. This one doesn't hold water, not from what we know about the people involved. Maybelle would have used the information and come after him later on, not now."

Lyle was right. Maybelle was the logical choice for his ex-wife.

"I still have work to do," Lyle said staring at me, as if he wasn't sitting in my chair in my office. I left, hopefully without a huff. Mark was at the desk when I came out. I caught him up on what was going on and then headed out to my apartment.

The downstairs was quieter, though not quiet. A number of people still stood around in the main basement lobby area and others were in the conference room. I saw Nell working inside, talking to several people. She didn't look up at me and another person quickly grabbed her for more questions.

She might know if Frank and Maybelle had been married but she was so busy, I doubted she'd appreciate the interruption. I'd leave that to Lyle. Assuming he thought of questioning her. It was quiet down at the end of the corridor near my place.

My apartment felt chilly and I checked the heat. I had lowered it a bit to save energy when we went on the generator. I turned it up a little bit. Chai and Latte were curled together so tightly it was difficult to tell where one cat ended and the other began. Latte had rooted himself under the afghan which was now at least partially covering both of them.

Neither of them meowed at me when I entered, but I did get the stink-eye from Chai, probably because the apartment was cooler than they liked.

My windows weren't ice covered, and looking out over the back, I was pleased that it appeared to have almost stopped snowing. I saw a few flurries but those could have come from the wind blowing a bit of snow off the roof as easily as from the storm. I hoped it was just a little wind and that the storm was over, though it was doubtful. Looking closer, there were far too many flurries to just have come from the wind. Still, even if it hadn't stopped, it was hopefully a light enough snow that the plows would make a difference and emergency vehicles could get here soon.

I settled in to do reports. I recalled that there were two writers close to Maybelle's room. Diana something and Laura Wells. I noodled the idea that one of them could have been working with Frank. Maybe they knew him. Or maybe one of them was Frank's ex and he got the wrong room.

But that wasn't right because Maybelle wasn't murdered in her room. She was murdered downstairs. So, Frank wouldn't need the room until he tried to kill Melissa, if Frank was the killer.

Unable to settle, I grabbed my keys. I needed to find Diane and Laura. One or both of them could have been injured or killed so that the murderer could have waited in the room for Melissa. I was halfway down the hallway when Olive appeared.

I told her what I was thinking. She popped out and was back in seconds.

"No bodies in either room. Both rooms are clean so housekeeping has been there. If he hurt either woman, then he didn't leave them in their room," Olive reported.

I paused and sighed. It had seemed like such a good idea.

"Well, there goes that theory," I said.

"You'll have another bright idea. I had no idea Frank was connected to this. He's just the sort you'd expect to be a killer, though, isn't he? A rather irritating and annoying man." Olive shuddered.

"Supposedly he writes horror. Probably because he is one," I said. I turned back and walked slowly to the apartment. I had soup in the refrigerator. I could have that for lunch. The cats would appreciate the company, at least a little, even if I was having a hard time focusing.

Olive playfully swatted at me. If she hit me, I only felt a slight chill.

"You quite liked that horror writer from Canada exploring haunted hotels on his way south," Olive said. "And the other guy, the one from out west? He was nice too. And the Canadian women. Why, I can think of half a dozen people who write horror that you quite like."

"But not Frank," I said, unlocking my apartment. The cats looked up at me, annoyed at being disturbed again.

"Some people are just difficult," Olive said.

"And his friend, Paul. Did you know he purposely misled Suzanne about who he was?" I said.

"I was there," Olive said. "In the office. Watching. I don't think either of them saw me, but I was there. I got the impression he was play acting because he wanted to know what Suzanne knew more than anything."

"So he was nosey but didn't want to ask questions?" I frowned. It seemed like a weird way to get answers.

Olive shrugged, lifting her hands up. "That was just my impression. Maybe he worried about people seeing him as being too interested in the case? I mean, if he knows Frank, then perhaps he knows what Frank did."

"Or he helped him," I said. "He seemed almost eager to talk to Lyle, though."

Olive frowned. "I ought to go find him. He didn't see me when I listened in. If he's alone I can appear and he'll never know I'm not alive."

"Let me know if you find anything out," I said.

Olive disappeared and I sighed. I didn't feel any closer to finding the murderer than I had earlier. I should have asked Olive to listen in on Diana and Laura, too. In case they were involved and not dead, but it was too late. Olive would show up when she felt like it.

I heard a bunch of screams down the hallway. I quickly locked the door and hurried down the hall. Several people were standing by the dorm door, looking down the hallway, frowning.

"You don't suppose that was Clara, *again*?" someone asked.

Personally, I hoped it was Clara again rather than someone else getting murdered or attacked.

When I got out to the main lobby area, all the writers there were talking at once.

"What is it?" I asked.

"We thought we saw Maybelle!" one of them said.

"She hustled out of the room where she died and went towards the conference room!" another said.

"I thought I heard her moaning!" another said.

Maybelle was not someone that I wanted to have haunting the hotel as a ghost. Until I saw her myself, I'd reserve judgement. Particularly since none of our usual ghosts went around moaning. However, this was potentially the second time someone had seen her heading out of the hallway where she'd died. You'd have thought her ghost would have gone to the stairs, but she didn't go that far.

Ghosts didn't always follow the same route. Clara was really the only one who was habitual about it. Angus could appear at any of the windows. He'd probably looked in on us through the ice, though everything was so covered, no one had noticed him. Poor man. I wondered if that's what had happened to him when he died.

Smithers could show up anywhere in the restaurant and at any time, though shortly before a storm was the most likely time to see him. Olive ended up wherever she wanted and she spoke. Smithers didn't speak, but he was known to randomly point, which used to scare the person he pointed at, as if they were certain they were the next to die.

Several of them had written blogs about it and years later they'd post that they'd avoided the Smither's "curse." Other than Maybelle, the only potential ghost I hadn't seen was the one in room 785. When this was over, I might have to go up and stay there, just to see if there really was a ghost. Although Frank sounded disappointed enough that he hadn't run into one.

No more screams, but plenty of talking. I walked down the hallway. It felt normal. Clara's chill normally lasted a bit longer. Not so much that I'd notice if I weren't looking for a chill but if, like now, I were testing it, I'd feel something. No chill.

Someone could be playing a prank. I heard something fall in the Skyler room. I'd been concentrating on other things and I jumped. The security person sitting outside the room did, too. We both looked at each other, wondering what might be going on.

"Did you see the supposed ghost?" I asked.

"It started further down the hall," he said. "And to be honest, I was playing a game."

I nodded. No harm done.

I used my key to unlock the door and look inside. The room appeared empty. No one had cleaned up the blood on the carpet. We'd need a specialty cleaner for that. Actually, I'd probably try and get the carpet replaced. The room still had the general stink of death. The conversations out in the main lobby seemed very far away.

Normally, I am not afraid of ghosts but this wasn't like our normal hauntings and I peered around with trepidation, half expecting the cadaverous Frank to jump out and terrify me. Or perhaps his companion, Paul. At least with the latter, I'd probably have Olive to help me out and distract him.

But nothing happened. I didn't even notice what had fallen at first, but then I saw that one of the chairs had fallen to the side and hit the wall. It had to have been what we heard. I just couldn't explain how it had happened.

Chapter Twenty-Three

I tried to breathe in deeply to calm myself, but the room still had that metallic stink and undertones of something worse. I had to get out of there. The colors seemed too bright and the room began to spin slowly. My stomach lurched.

One good thing about not having time to eat was that I didn't think I'd vomit much if something did come up. And well, in this room, the carpet needed replacing anyway.

Closer to the door, the sounds of the writers reached me. Talking and laughing. Footsteps pounding up the stairwell to the main level. I left the room and stood near the security guard. He glanced up at me, worried.

"Are you okay?"

"I think so, now," I said, though I had no real idea. My heart was still beating way too fast and my chest felt tight. I wondered if I was having a heart attack, but it didn't feel all that painful. Besides, I was in good health. Had had a wellness check not three months before when the doctor had told me that my heart was strong and I was in good condition, taking no medications.

Perhaps someone had put something in the room, some sort of poison. Except someone would have had to get in there to place the poison.

Calmer, now, I decided I had probably had a panic attack. Irritated with myself for not having more fortitude, I glanced back at the room.

"You can lock the room back up," I said. "I don't think anything has been moved. A chair fell and it may have been placed awkwardly and something upstairs may have caused the walls to vibrate just enough that it fell."

The guard nodded, though he still looked rather worried.

"I'm going to head back upstairs and talk to Mark." I don't know why I said that. Perhaps it was to reassure him. Maybe it was to reassure myself.

When I got to the basement lobby, where the stairs called me, and the elevators had small groups standing in front of them, I found that the one thing I really wanted to do was hurry down to my apartment and hide under the covers. I liked to think of myself as unflappable, but I guess a murder and an attack were more than my usual managerial skills could handle.

The stairs still seemed like the best deal. The security person might see me heading down the wrong hallway and become more concerned. Further, the way I felt, I might just drop into my bed and take a nap. The cats certainly wouldn't be unhappy with me if I did that.

Resolutely, I placed my hand on the metal banister and started up the stairwell, pausing when I got to the landing halfway up. I took a few deep breaths. I wasn't breathless, but it felt good to pause and get my bearings again. My heart rate seemed more appropriate to what it should be.

My legs were holding up and not shaking. Maybe I just needed movement.

And probably food.

I waved at the reception desk and headed to the café to grab a sandwich. I wasn't all that hungry, but got something anyway, forcing myself to eat. I'd been living on coffee and the soup I'd planned for lunch had never gotten made because I'd let my thoughts interrupt me.

Finishing my food in the café, surrounded by writers and other guests, I took my plate to the back so there was one less thing for the girl wiping tables to do. Before I even got back out from behind the counter, someone else had grabbed the table and was looking at a menu. I hoped they all ordered plenty of food. Cold weather tended to do that. I hadn't checked the inventories yet.

Maybe Lyle would be out of my office and I could work upstairs. I had no desire to be alone with the cats. I had visions of Frank as a killer breaking down my door and stabbing me repeatedly. The boys would probably have hidden safely under the bed before he even got in. Then I'd lie there, in my blood. Chai would probably taste it and decide if it was worth eating. Latte would likely sit upon me until my body went cold.

I shook my head, getting that morbid image out of it and headed back to the desk. Mark and Suzanne were both there. I noticed a plate from the café on the desk. Normally I asked workers not to eat behind the desk but this was an unusual situation. I was glad someone had thought to make sure Suzanne wasn't alone.

"Have we heard anything new?" I asked, eyeing the closed door of my office.

Mark shook his head.

Suzanne did the same seconds later.

"Lyle in there with someone or is he just working alone?" I asked.

"I think he's alone for now," Mark said. "I heard him call the forensics guys a few minutes ago. They're all chomping at the bit to get out. We have a couple of guests hoping they can make it out as well, though I doubt the roads will be that clear."

"Are any of them potential suspects?" I asked.

"I don't have a clue who's a suspect and who isn't. One of them stayed on the fourth floor and is named Laura Wells. I guess she's a bit claustrophobic and she really just wants to get out. She's been down here looking out the window multiple times and asking if I knew when the roads would be clear. I asked her why because her reservation is through the weekend which is why I know about the claustrophobia. The others are all people who were supposed to leave today and didn't change their reservations, checking on roads and what to do if they aren't clear," Mark said.

Laura Wells again. If only we had internet.

"Laura Wells' room is nearly across from the murdered woman's," Suzanne said.

I nodded. Mark looked surprised.

"I wish we knew more about her," I said.

"She seemed perfectly nice," Mark said. "Not young. Gray haired. Long hair pulled back in a single braid. She had on decent clothing for the weather except she was in jeans. At least she had boots and a sweater."

I recalled the woman downstairs with Kendra and Melissa. She could be one of their friends. I wondered about Diane. She could be the other friend. Of course, she hadn't been begging to leave.

If Laura had anything to do with the murders, though, it would be odd for her to bring attention to herself. Her insistence upon leaving didn't fit with the premeditation of the earlier events. The filed steak knives had taken some doing.

"I'm going to go check on Melissa," I said. I held out little hope that Petra was still there. She'd been nodding off hours ago. Jake would probably have spelled her or perhaps Paul, the one we knew was a forensic tech with medical background and not the man pretending to be him.

I walked down the hallway and around the corner to the med center. Melissa was still asleep. Jake was there, making notes on a heavy-duty tablet.

"Any change?" I asked.

"Not that I can tell. Petra filled me in on her evening before she went off to catch a bit of sleep. Are we compensating her?" he asked.

"I'll comp her rooms." I could do that as soon as I got to a computer. Maybe I could kick Lyle out of the office and send him down here. It seemed quiet enough. Or maybe he could work in the security office.

Jake nodded and glanced over at Melissa. "The strange thing I found is that most of her wounds weren't terribly deep. Only a couple of them required stitches and one of those was a head wound, which bleed like a bitch. I don't know why she hasn't woken up yet, but everything I can check says her vitals are good."

"Do you think the blood fooled our killer?" I asked.

"From what I understand Maybelle was killed by having her throat slit. Someone who can do that knows what they're doing. Melissa was out but her throat wasn't slit. It seems a little sloppy."

"Do you think it's someone else?" I asked.

"Same sort of weapon," Jake said. "I suppose it could be two people working together, but..."

I nodded, knowing what he meant. That didn't make sense.

Just then Olive appeared. Jake jumped. She grinned at him.

"Hello Jake," she said evenly.

Jake nodded at her, scooting his chair back a little. He didn't seem afraid so much as intimidated.

"Did you find anything out?" I asked.

"I spent some time with Paul at the main restaurant. It's not terribly crowded despite all the writers. I'm sure many of them were scared off by the snow. Too bad for Frank. Smithers was marching around there, which Paul seemed fascinated by," Olive said. "He even used one of those little phones with the camera to film it."

"Did you just watch or did you talk to him?" I asked.

"Oh, I talked to him. He thought I was another guest trying to pick him up," Olive said, giggling a little. She even brought a hand to the ends of her short hair.

I smiled at her. In her day, Olive had probably been a lovely woman. She was a nice-looking woman even on the day she died and I had a feeling that wasn't her best.

"Anyway, he told me that he'd been hoping to see Smithers. I asked if he were there with friends and he said he'd come alone and that his friend Frank had invited himself, making out like he was a ghost hunter when he just writes horror novels. I guess Paul, while he's a tech, dabbles in ghost hunting. I heard more than I wanted to about paranormal conventions. Have you ever heard of such a thing?" Olive stared at me.

"I have," I said easily. "In fact, you might remember that we hosted some here in years past. We had all those people walking around with the boxes trying to get a fix on where you guys were. Clara didn't bother to show herself once and I'm not sure Smithers did, either."

"I seem to recall that," Olive said. She didn't look happy. "Paul didn't have one of those boxes, though, thank heavens. But he told me about stuff. Bigfoot and all of that as well. He thinks there might be something like Bigfoot in our mountains!"

Olive seemed offended by that last, though I wasn't sure why.

I shrugged. "Did you find anything more out about who Frank might have been married to?"

"He wasn't interested in talking about Frank. It was all the paranormal stuff. Now that I think about it, he almost seemed eager to have Melissa die to see if her ghost stayed in the hotel. Which is really a horrible thing. I told him that the hotel had had more deaths than ghosts so not everyone stayed behind." Olive sniffed a bit.

We were lucky we'd had as few deaths as we'd had, but even then, I couldn't image the place if every single person having died there stayed on. Ghosts all had their reasons for staying. I sometimes thought that perhaps Clara wasn't a ghost the way Olive was and that she was sort of a reflection of the girl's terror right before she'd died. Olive didn't believe me so I didn't bring it up again, but I still thought so. She didn't act like either Olive or Smithers who seemed to have some control over what they did.

The most control I'd seen from Clara was when she winked at me. Given that Clara seemed to do the same thing over and over again, I wondered if Olive had been able to get through to her. Perhaps she was a ghost like the others but so terrified that her only thought upon appearing was to run away.

"Did you learn anything other than he's obsessed about the paranormal?" I asked.

"Not really. I don't know that he had anything to do with this. He seems like he's a bit of a jerk, rather full of himself and potentially mean, but I couldn't find how he might be connected to one of the writers. Unless Frank was married to one, but that didn't come up." Olive huffed.

"We've learned that Laura Wells wants to leave the hotel as soon as possible. She's a writer and her room is right across from Maybelle's," I said. "If she has computer skills, she'd be perfect to have attacked Melissa."

"I'll go up and see what I can find out. But if she's in her room, then I can't just pop in there." Then Olive grinned. "I mean, I could, but I haven't ever done that. It might be fun."

Then she popped out, leaving me in the med center with Jake.

"I have to say, I wonder if we can put Olive on the security staff at the hotel. Can you imagine the stuff she could find out?" Jake said quietly.

"I think she'd see it as a demotion," I said.

Jake looked slightly offended. Then I gave him a look. "She had my job before she died. Did it well for years, although the hotel was floundering. That wasn't her fault. The owners expanded too much too fast. No one thought that the northern North Carolina Appalachians might not be the kind of place that drew people wanting a spa and resort experience. There isn't even a golf course."

At one time, there had been talk of adding one, but the area wasn't flat enough to have any decent greens and that idea had been dropped. They'd talked about building a ski resort, but this week excepted, we really didn't get that much snow. There were two other ski areas within a short driving distance. Another one didn't make financial sense.

Instead, they'd added some hiking trails and the owners had talked about putting in a small tubing park for kids in the winter. They thought maybe they could even create one of the summer snow tubing parks as well. I'd looked into those and I wasn't sure we were the perfect location for it, but what did I know? I'd only increased the receipts by offering guests the possibility of a haunted hotel experience.

Jake nodded. "I guess coming to work for someone else would feel like a come down, then, wouldn't it."

"And Olive is very proud of her work, too," I said. "I suspect she's still around because she loved what she was doing and couldn't imagine moving on to something else."

At least I hoped that was why she was still around. I'd hate to be stuck at the hotel forever, trying to manage things through the humans on staff and losing touch as things changed over the years. As I got older and reflected on my own mortality, I had to admit that not dying might be nice. I appreciated knowing there was something after. However, I didn't really want to hang around this place forever, limited on where I could go.

"Man, I hope I'm never that attached to a job," Jake laughed, echoing my thoughts.

I took another look at Melissa, wishing she'd wake. I wanted to know if she had seen who had attacked her. She probably had to have. She at least had to know who had lured her to the room.

"I wish she'd wake enough for us to question her," I said.

"Now that she's more stable, I'm hoping that she'll be able to tell us something before everyone starts leaving. At least the writers have a reason to stay for a few more days and they're our most likely suspects," Jake said. He looked back down at his tablet again.

I left him to his work and walked back down towards the desk, my mind still full of ideas about who could have done this.

Chapter Twenty-Four

Lyle was still in my office, so I headed back downstairs to my apartment to attempt to focus and get something done. The afternoon was wearing on and while the plow had disappeared, no one seemed to be going anywhere. Our phone lines still weren't working reliably, which bothered me. Cell service continued to be non-existent.

When I got to my apartment and found I'd opened the container of soup and left it on the counter, only to be knocked over by nosey cats, I was near tears. I hadn't remembered opening it, I was so frazzled. When I finished cleaning, I looked out the window and saw the snow still drifting down, harder than it had been earlier. Our storm hadn't quite left us. Then I really did sit down and cry.

I was tired and overwhelmed at dealing with something I had no training in, yet felt obligated to do to help my guests. My office had been taken over. My apartment smelled of chicken and rice and I needed to do a thorough mopping to make sure I got everything. Finally, my boys didn't even come out of the bedroom to comfort me.

Granted, it did feel cooler than it should in the apartment. I looked at my heat. At some point it had been turned back down. I frowned. I couldn't remember doing that.

I looked around the place, noticing my book was out of place on the end table. I walked slowly into my bedroom, hoping to find Chai and Latte curled on the bed, perhaps glaring at me for not getting a better soup, but they weren't there. I squatted down by the bed and saw them peering out at me.

Neither of them gave a peep, which should have warned me something was wrong.

I stood up and looked around the room. My water glass on the nightstand had been moved. All these things could have been done by the cats but it wasn't likely to have happened on the same day.

I went back out and looked at my computer. I'd foolishly left it on. The screen saver was on, but I'd been back for some time, cleaning and what not. Someone could have looked at what I was doing. I got a chill down my back as I spent a moment trying to remember what I'd been doing before I left.

I ought to leave, but I didn't want to leave my boys with a murderer. If they were willing to harm people, what would they do to my cats?

Torn, I stood there.

Finally, I turned towards the door, thinking that perhaps I'd just leave the door open. The cats could flee if necessary and I'd catch them later. The staff knew I had Siamese. At the very least, it would tell someone that there was trouble down there.

I barely fumbled with the lock when I heard one board on the floor squeak. I started to turn but something hit me across the side of the head and I fell. The door remained closed.

If only I had thought sooner, perhaps I could have gotten it open.

"If you were really astute and wanted to cover your tracks, you would have closed up your computer and erased your search history. You were looking into Laura Wells," a woman's voice said.

I rubbed the side of my head, intending to turn over and see who it was. The dispassion in the voice was familiar to me, but focusing was difficult.

A foot stopped my roll, keeping me staring at the bottom of the door I hadn't been able to open.

If I died a violent death in the hotel, I worried I'd end up like poor Clara. No matter that I was certain she was just sort of shadow of strong emotion, perhaps such a thing would tie part of my spirit to this place forever. I wouldn't even have Olive's freedom to wander around the hotel.

Instead, my shade would forever lay on the floor by the door screaming. Or whatever it was I would do before I was finally murdered by this woman.

"Are you Laura?" I asked.

A bark of a laugh. "Hell no. I ought to have killed the bitch because she knows I wanted to use her room." Again, the voice was familiar. Dispassionate, even with the expletive. Like someone trying to care but not quite doing so.

"You were on track, interviewing Frank," the voice said again. "But then you got smart. No one was supposed to know the name on that room and connect it to me. I spent a great deal of time making sure she was the one who asked for a room down that way and the bitch just didn't understand. But finally, she agreed to ask for a room close to the stairs. Maybelle always does."

I listened to the pause. There was more to the story, but she wasn't saying.

"I had to use the fact that I needed to get back at Frank to get her to do it. And now she's all about fleeing, drawing attention. Stupid bitch." The final words were more disgust than anger.

"Who was Frank to you?" I asked.

"My ex-husband. He tried to steal my writing ideas. Tried to steal everyone's ideas in hopes of writing a book that people wanted to read. He's a poor writer. Can't think like a real person, he's too self-absorbed. If he could get his head out of his behind, he'd see that that creepy friend of his hates him every bit as much as everyone else."

I managed to turn my head a bit to see Kendra. I frowned. That was not who I was expecting. She'd seemed dependent upon her sister, and yet Melissa was lying in a room unconscious, her body covered in cuts, some large enough to potentially have killed her.

"Kendra?" I whispered.

She looked down at me. "Surprised?"

I didn't know what to say. I hadn't expected her to have harmed her sister. "But Melissa?"

"She did that to herself," Kendra said. "Literally. I made Laura get the room across from Maybelle so I could make sure no one was around when I went in to give her the drugs that would knock her out so everyone would think her wounds were worse than they were."

"Why Maybelle? And why would we believe Frank would murder Maybelle?" I asked.

"Oh, there's plenty of reason. Considering Maybelle's newest manuscript that she's shopping is a bit more of a horror tale. Just enough romance to make it one of hers. And guess who wrote the horror part of it? That's right. Frankie boy. He was asking her for feedback, probably to piss me off because I can't stand Maybelle, not that anyone can. And suddenly, his plot ideas get written in her own hand with a romance thrown in. Typical Maybelle. Lift huge portions of the good stuff word for word, do a bit of editing or redrafting on the not-so-good stuff and add in a little something. By the time an editor got through smoothing out the romance plot so that it actually fit the manuscript, even Frank wouldn't have recognized his work," Kendra said.

"But that wouldn't exactly be plagiarism, would it?" I didn't understand that much about writing.

"She was lifting huge parts of a manuscript word for word, with the same general plot, though she threw in a huge romance plot. It certainly is plagiarism," Kendra snapped. "She did it to me once."

"What did you do?" I asked.

"I called her on it. Made a stink. She countersued. Said because I only had part of the manuscript, I was the one plagiarizing her!" Kendra snarled.

She stamped the foot that was pushing against my back, easing up. I tried to roll a little further from her, but almost immediately, she put her foot back on my shoulder. Not like I was going to roll out the door anyway.

"So you killed her, hoping to make it look like Frank did it," I paraphrased.

"Figured it would kill two birds with one stone. When Frank was complaining about having to talk to the police, I thought I'd won."

"How did you get him here?" I asked.

"Oh heck. Paul had this on the agenda a long time ago. I knew Frank would eventually follow and probably spend way too much money. I made sure Nell kept hearing about this place. Then I mentioned this place online in the groups the paranormal cozy writers frequent. It only took a little nudging suggestion that we come here and all of them were practically begging Nell to arrange it," Kendra said. "Easy peasy. Of course, Frank took longer to commit, so that was a bit scary."

"And what did you do to your sister?" I asked.

"Nothing. Like I said. She did that herself. To take suspicion off of me and put it on Frank. Melissa and Frank had quite the fraught relationship. After what he did to me and the way he treated me, Melissa hated him. Actually, she hated him before that, but that's neither here nor there. Just that she was right about him and I was wrong. I'm just not a particularly social person, so I didn't see the red flags she saw."

I tried to pull away but Kendra stamped down harder on my back. I cried out.

"Excuse me," I heard Olive say. Leave it to her to try and be polite when addressing a murderer.

I felt Kendra whirl. The foot was gone. I rolled up onto my hands and knees while Kendra slashed at Olive. It went right through her. Olive stood there looking at Kendra sadly.

"What the hell?" Kendra said.

"The ghosts here are real," I reminded her. "This is Olive."

Kendra turned to glare at me. "I don't know what sort of trick this is…"

I stared at her.

"The camera image is so solid. Not like what we did with Maybelle, which I thought was pretty good," Kendra whispered. She moved a hand closer to Olive, touching the image, sinking one finger slowly into Olive's arm. Kendra pulled back and stared.

Olive just raised her eyebrows and gave her a look that said nothing so much as 'so what.'

Kendra stepped back and whirled on me. Her knife was out. The sharp point glinted in the light. She must have prepared a set of them or something. No one could have sharpened that many knives that much once they got here.

"You've visited the Inn before," I said.

"I came to do reconnaissance. Last year. As soon as I knew the conference would be here. Only spent the afternoon. I didn't want to become a regular guest in case you have something that links us. Too much notice."

"Killing me will get you noticed," I said.

"No one knows," Kendra said.

"I do," Olive said. "And I talk. A lot. To everyone. In fact, I talked to Lyle a few minutes ago, when I saw Maggie on the floor."

I felt a wave of relief sweep over me. Lyle was coming. Hopefully, he'd bring Jake. Hopefully, Jake would have something to defend himself with and Lyle would have his gun.

"I doubt it," Kendra said. "Melissa and I timed the drugs. She should be coming around about now and he'll be busy getting her statement. And if not, she knows what to do."

I had a feeling whatever it was Melissa was supposed to do wasn't a good thing.

It might be up to me and Olive to get me out of this alive. I hoped we were up to it!

Chapter Twenty-Five

Kendra looked between me and Olive. I could tell she still wasn't certain what was going on with Olive. Still, her stance with the knife was solid. My back was to the door. I took a step to the side and Kendra advanced a larger step, bringing the stainless steel of the knife far too close to my face.

I leaned my head back without stepping back. I smelled Kendra's faint pungent body odor along with the stink of my spilled soup that hadn't dissipated. I heard the wind outside rattling the windows. The snow had slowed down again allowing me a view of the trees and the fact that the clouds didn't appear quite as thick as they had been.

The knife that Kendra was now edging down towards my throat made it difficult to breathe in very deeply.

"You're just going to mess this up," Olive said suddenly.

I jumped slightly, feeling the brush of metal against my chin. Kendra really was too close. Unfortunately, she didn't jump at all when Olive spoke.

"The only way out of this apartment is through the employee area. There are plenty of people in the dorms going in and out all the time, mostly past the apartment. Someone will see you. There are also cameras down this hallway and no hiding places to avoid them. Even if they miss you going out, they'll find you on the camera. They'll know who killed Maggie and that won't go well for you," Olive said.

"You should have just stayed with the original plan and hoped to get out of here with your sister and the paramedics before anyone was the wiser. You could have knocked Maggie over the head and put her to bed, for instance. Maybe even tied her up, loosely, of course. Taken her keys and locked her door."

Olive began to pace, running her fingers through the pearls that lay at her neck.

"Yes, that could have worked. No one would have been looking at what was going on until after you were gone. You could even have been out of the country if you got to Charlotte or Dulles in time."

Olive looked at Kendra.

"But no, you had to go and decide you liked killing. You do, don't you?"

Kendra didn't answer.

Olive didn't seem to mind. She just nodded to herself. "So why was your friend Laura so eager to get out of here?"

"She's a bitch, like I said," Kendra said. "And she knew enough to start putting pieces together and disliked how she might be implicated."

"How very interesting," Olive said. "Do you write these types of stories? This all seems very well thought out."

Kendra started to give an explanation and then glared at Olive. "You're just stalling."

She'd moved fractionally closer to Olive. I took a chance and took another step to the side, towards the kitchen. I had knives there. Maybe I could get to them.

Kendra must have had eyes in the back of her head, she whirled on me so fast. However, I'd taken a small step, so she couldn't be sure I'd actually moved. Her eyes narrowed and she stepped further back so that she could watch both me and Olive.

It wasn't ideal but at least I could breathe again.

Of course, my heart was trying to race away. If Lyle were coming here, you'd think he could be a bit faster about it. I worried about what Melissa might have planned for upstairs to keep people from coming to my assistance.

Olive stood there, with her arms crossed. "Still waiting on an answer."

Kendra glared. Her knife seemed to sparkle in the dim light.

A particularly strong guest of wind hit the window and made a sound. I jumped.

Kendra didn't move. The woman had nerves of steel or she really did have eyes in the back of her head.

Kendra's right foot stepped towards me. I stared at the knife.

When she'd struck at Olive she'd gone left to right with her right hand. And low to high. The image was etched in my brain. If I ducked back correctly, I could avoid being injured.

At my age, that was a big if. I tried to breathe normally, but my chest wasn't having it, allowing only the smallest amount of air inside.

My hands were slippery with sweat. Even if I made to a drawer for a knife, I doubted my ability to hold onto one.

If I died right there, I worried about who would care for Latte and Chai. I had a sister in Portland and she could take them, but it was a very long trip. I hated the idea of them being put in carriers in the cargo hold of an airplane. I hated the very idea of them being separated. I needed to redo my will and make sure there was someone local to take the cats.

Olive couldn't look after them. She couldn't touch a food dish or open a can of cat food any more than they could. In a way, Olive wasn't that much different from a cat. Except she could talk. With words.

If I had time to wonder what that said about me, I probably would have, but Kendra was now close enough to make a slash.

She moved before I was really ready for it, but I was angled so that there was space for me to jump back. I landed in the kitchen.

My kitchen had always been an adequate galley area, with counters on either side. Two people could fit in there, barely. Not that I had guests in my kitchen often. Even when I did have guests, we ate at one of the restaurants. But I knew it was possible to squeeze two in there. If we liked each other.

However, I'd have to brush against Kendra to get out of the small area. She stood blocking the entrance, near where I'd stood, knife in hand.

The grin on her face told me she knew she had me cornered.

In getting away that one time, I'd just made my situation infinitely worse.

I took in my small space. The knife drawer was still a step behind me and on the side furthest from me. I'd have to take a step towards it and then pull it open, giving Kendra ample time to attack. On my side was the refrigerator and the sink. Unfortunately, I had no dirty knives lying in the sink. Even then, it was on my left, which is not my dominant hand.

She took a step and I opened the refrigerator door, pulling it towards me, using it as a shield. It was all I could think to do.

Kendra backed up to try and go around.

I threw the door towards her. She wasn't quite out of range of the swing and it hit her arm. Her left arm, unfortunately.

I backed up and got to the faucet, turning the hot water on high. I pulled the sprayer out of the main faucet and aimed it at Kendra's eyes.

She held up her hands to avoid the water.

She took a few more steps back.

I tried to pull the faucet further, but those things weren't meant to put out fires. They were meant to wash dishes. At the sink.

For the moment, we were at a stalemate. And my apartment was getting soaked.

Olive applauded.

Kendra was back beyond the door. I couldn't rush her, though. She was still closer to it than I was. Maybe I could reach a drawer for my own knife.

Olive glided towards the window, looking out, making it more difficult for Kendra to keep an eye on both of us. It was about time the ghost did more than watch.

I stepped back, still holding the water and grabbed a random knife out of the drawer. I waved it at her with my right hand while my left sprayed water.

Just then the door banged open.

Lyle stood there, a gun in his hand.

He looked first in my direction, causing me to drop the sprayer, which fortunately shrank back into the sink.

Then around to Kendra.

She tried to rush him.

Lyle didn't fire. He didn't have to. Wayne was there to rush her before she got anywhere close to him.

He grabbed her arm easily and brought it up. Then he twisted it until she dropped the knife.

Lyle quickly got out handcuffs and pulled her arms behind her.

I shut off the water and breathed out. We'd found our killer.

Chapter Twenty-Six

I breathed heavily, though I hadn't been moving. My body felt as if I had been running for hours. My hands shook and I set down my knife, not wanting to hurt anyone with it.

Olive glided over to me while Lyle was reading Kendra her rights.

"I have no idea what you thought you'd do with a bread knife," she said looking down at the knife on the counter.

I'd grabbed my high-end bread cutting knife, a lovely thing with a serrated edge and a beautiful wooden handle that I'd gotten as a gift long ago. It stayed sharp, but the rounded tip at the end probably wouldn't have been good for stabbing and the edge was meant for slicing not for stabbing or cutting.

"I just grabbed one randomly," I said.

"Next time you should glance at what you grab. That cleaver in there would have been much more threatening."

"It's not sharp. I haven't used it in years. There's not really a need but it's not that big, so…" I shrugged.

"A cleaver doesn't need to be sharp. The person you're waving it at doesn't know it lacks an edge. It looks threatening though. A lot more threatening than the sharpest of bread knives. I mean, what were you going to do? Make her a sandwich?"

Olive moved off with that comment.

Lyle was standing up and looking at me.

"What took you so long? Olive said she talked to you quite a while ago," I said. I leaned against the counter. Now that they knew I wasn't in danger, my legs were threatening not to hold me up.

"Kendra had come to see Melissa, just briefly. They barely touched and then she was gone. About five minutes later, Melissa came out of her stupor and attacked Jake," Lyle said. "At some point, she'd found a scalpel and did a number on his arms and shoulders before he got her under control. I had to be there to read her her rights, which only took a minute. It's not like I was going to leave you here to be murdered by her sister."

Lyle seemed indignant that I thought he took too long. The time I'd spent in my apartment with Kendra seemed to have lasted hours. I felt dizzy.

To his credit, seeing me hanging my head, Lyle stepped over and escorted me to the sofa, taking baby steps around the apartment. Wayne had Kendra well in hand and she wasn't saying a word now that she had a bigger audience.

"I think she needs some water," Olive said when Lyle stepped back, about to ask me what I needed.

"And maybe a cookie," Olive added. "Or something like that. She's had a fright. They say chamomile tea is wonderful for a fright, but I've never been a fan. Water is good. And perhaps a decaf tea of some sort. Maybe a bit of spice. I always liked a bit of spiciness in my teas."

Lyle stared at her for a moment. He stepped around

the puddled water and got me a glass. He looked in the kitchen for something to eat and found a piece of cheese.

It's not that I had nothing else in the apartment, but most things required some level of cooking. Cookies were not on the menu when I was home alone, unless I purchased a single one from the café or when I was out in town.

Wayne took Kendra out. She stomped her feet through the wet spots on the floor. I needed to clean that up.

"I'll go tell housekeeping you need someone to mop a large spill," Olive said before she disappeared leaving me and Lyle alone.

"Are you going to be okay?" he asked. "I need to get up there."

I nodded. "I'm not quite sure I want to be completely alone, though. Could you grab someone from the dorm?"

Lyle nodded. He opened the door and I noticed a half dozen employees standing in the hallway looking first at Wayne pushing a woman in handcuffs in front of him and then at Lyle coming out of my apartment and me on the sofa. Chances were, he was going to have a more difficult time getting only one person to come to my aid rather than all of them, which, I thought was more company than I could possibly handle.

Olive popped back in and shooed Lyle out of the apartment. Dori, one of my restaurant workers, was chosen to sit with me. She was a wiry young woman who competed in martial art tournaments. She was well known around the town for her abilities. No doubt that had something to do with Lyle's decision to send her in.

"What happened?" she asked, staring at the water on the floor.

"Kendra thought that Maggie was onto something and decided to try and attack her. I was about to appear and let her know what I'd found out when I saw things and I popped up to let Lyle and Jake know. Apparently, just after that, Melissa attacked Jake, making Lyle wait." Olive huffed as if that was the most ridiculous thing.

"And then Maggie got herself trapped in the kitchen. At first, she tried to bean Kendra with the refrigerator door and when that didn't work, she sprayed her with the kitchen sprayer. It's probably all out of whack, now," Olive went on.

"And then, she tried to defend herself with a bread knife. We were lucky that Lyle came in just then and put a stop to it. Maggie could definitely stand to learn a few of your martial art moves," Olive said.

I glanced over at the ghost, surprised at what she kept up on with the workers.

"Hey. That's more than a lot of people would have done," Dori said quietly. She patted my knee. I smiled at her, hoping to ignore Olive's commentary that made me sound like someone in a slapstick comedy show.

Pretty soon someone from housekeeping arrived to clean up the water. Latte meowed from the bedroom. While the cats were annoyed, at least they were safe. I needed to check on them. I stood up, but felt dizzy.

Upon learning what I needed, Dori helped me to the bedroom where I peered under the bed. Both cats immediately came out and gave me a long going over. It wasn't a cookie, but almost as good.

Chapter Twenty-Seven

The next day, things were getting back to normal. The police had shown up not long after the plow had made it to the main road, which was already somewhat cleared. While this kind of ice storm is unusual for this area, we get enough snow that there were plows that could handle the regular snow.

Kendra and Melissa had been taken into custody. I sat with one of the detectives for some time telling him what Kendra had told me when she held me at knife point. Naturally, I left Olive out of the conversation, which wasn't all that easy given how Olive had distracted her. I had to tell him I kept asking questions that kept her talking.

I hoped that Olive hadn't lied about not being able to hear when she wasn't visible. She would not have liked me taking credit for her distractions. Of course, she'd been in my position and I'm sure she'd have known that the police weren't likely to take me seriously if I talked about ghosts.

Lyle backed me up. Fortunately, during our wait for the police, which wasn't all that long, we had time to get our non-ghost stories straight.

I was eating a large lunch at the café. It seems that nearly dying and being scared out of my skin worked up an appetite, at least once I'd gotten some rest. I'd barely been able to keep down soup the night before. That day, I had a French dip with fries and a side salad and planned to have one of little chocolate lava cakes for dessert.

"The thing I don't understand," Suzanne started, while having lunch with me. Everyone wanted to keep an eye on me after my near murder and Mark had insisted someone join me in the café. Suzanne was younger than I would have picked for a companion, but it was nice to have a meal with someone, though I would have preferred we not talk about the murders. We had a nice table for four in the back corner, away from the kitchen door. It was less desirable unless folks wanted privacy and privacy was not something our current guests appeared to want.

I eyed Suzanne's chef's salad with a critical eye. Some of the lettuce was just starting to wilt. I didn't like that at the inn.

"What?" I asked when I swallowed a bite of my sandwich. The thick pile of thin-sliced beef with cheese, onions and mushrooms was fantastic even without a bit of dip. I made sure not to drip on the pristine white table cloth. I knew it would be changed out later, but I hated to make more of a mess than I needed to.

"Didn't she say something about how it looked different than what they had done with Maybelle? Did they set up a ghost downstairs?" Suzanne asked.

"When we talked to Nell, she said that yes, a number of people had seen Maybelle rushing down the hall the day I heard screams down there. Apparently, Melissa and Kendra had set up some sort of video of her so that it appeared she was a ghost. They wanted to capitalize on our reputation," I said. "It was a bit of a distraction, perhaps to make everyone think they'd seen Maybelle down there after she was already dead. And then they figured seeing her ghost would make it even harder to pinpoint the time she was killed, particularly since the snow storm was likely to make it hard to get a definitive time of death. They were most worried about their friends, Diana and Laura suspecting something. From what Kendra said, it sounds like Laura did."

Suzanne raised an eyebrow as she crunched on her salad.

"Maybelle really had gone running out of the room. Kendra had put up a sign with Maybelle's name and it said, "You're dead." Maybelle had expected to meet with an editor to pitch her latest book, the rip-off of Frank's novel, and the sign, along with the ghostly reputation had completely freaked her out. Melissa had removed the sign by the time Kendra got Maybelle back in the room, pretending the editor was waiting for her. Maybelle been dead long enough for them to change the shirts they were wearing—they'd even brought two of the same tops so that if one got blood on it, they could change!—before Diana and Laura came down looking for them. What Kendra didn't see was that she'd got a rip on the edge of the jeans she'd worn while killing Maybelle. The police were able to match that to a piece of fabric they found near the body."

"Wow!" Suzanne said. "They really thought this out."

"They wrote mysteries. I mean, Melissa did. Kendra didn't help any longer. Everyone thought she was just shy. She was actually really angry about what had happened with Maybelle."

Laughter rose from a table a few feet away. It was a large group, most of them writers. It didn't include Diana and Laura. They'd checked out as soon as they could after talking to the police. They were local enough that the police allowed it after running background checks. I suspected they were just so upset to discover their friends were murderers.

"I'd be mad if someone took my work," Suzanne said. "I mean, it has to take a lot of time to come up with a mystery and then write it all down."

"At least you can," Olive said, appearing in one of the other chairs at our table.

"What do you mean?" Suzanne asked. She leaned back a little, though that was the only sign that Olive had startled her.

I noticed a few people doing double takes, not sure where the third woman had come from, but most went on with their lunch. If people are always so oblivious to ghosts, then no wonder most people didn't see them. They just weren't noticed.

Goosebumps rose on my arms, though Olive never left quite as much of a cold spot as Clara. I wondered if it had to do with the emotional energy or whatever it was that drove a ghost. Perhaps we'd discuss it sometime.

"I'd love to write a mystery," Olive said. "Just think, it could be told from my point of view. I could fictionalize this whole incident. Unfortunately, I can't type."

"What about dictation?" Suzanne asked. "There are plenty of phone apps."

Great. Now Olive would want a phone.

"A phone app?" Olive asked.

The two spent some time talking about that. I had a feeling that in my time off, I might be cleaning up the things that the app didn't understand with Olive standing over me, giving me more direction than I either wanted or needed.

"I think it would be best if you did a slightly different mystery," I said. "Or it could get you in trouble."

"What are they going to do to me?" Olive asked. "It's not like they can make me leave here."

"You'd have to have someone to be your front person," I said. "And I can't do it. Nor would I want to because I'd be liable if someone sued you."

"I'd do it," Suzanne said. "The first monies would pay me to go over the transcription and do some light editing and then I could publish it for you."

"You?" Olive said. "You wouldn't find someone in New York?"

Suzanne shook her head. "I've been listening to some of the writer's conversations. I guess it's not that hard to start publishing things on your own. I think it'd be fun. You know I studied graphic design. I just couldn't find a job in that field. But I bet I could do covers. And formatting wouldn't be hard. Maybe after dinner, I'll go talk to some of the writers to find out where to start."

Olive looked interested. I smiled at my two friends. This could be a great partnership. At least something good had come out of the weekend.

"That's a perfect idea!" one of the writers at a table near the front shouted loudly enough to make everyone turn.

She didn't repeat the idea so no one knew what it was, but apparently it was perfect.

"I think that settles it." Olive looked pleased at her potential partnership with Suzanne. I hoped my front desk person knew what she was getting into.

About Bonnie Elizabeth

Bonnie Elizabeth could never decide what to do, so she wrote stories about amazing things and sometimes she even finished them.

While rejection stung her so badly in person, she spent most of her young life talking to cats and dogs rather than people, she was unusually resilient when it came to rejections on her writing, racking up a good number of them.

Floating through a variety of jobs, including veterinary receptionist, cemetery administrator, and finally acupuncturist, she continued to write stories.

When the internet came along (yes she's old), she started blogging as her cat, because we all know cats don't notice rejection. Then she started publishing.

Bonnie writes in a variety of genres. Her popular Whisper series is contemporary fantasy and her Teenage Fairy Godmother series is written for teens. She has been published in a number of anthologies and is working on expanding her writing repertoire.

She lives with her husband (who talks less than she does) and her three cats, who always talk back.

Stay in Touch

Taken by the Sound

An Air of Suspicion

Little Dog Lost

Death Interrupted

Down in Whisper

A Haunting Whisper

A Haunting Attraction

Secrets Not Whispers

Only Human

Other Novels

One Bad Wish

Sun Spot Magic

Ghosts from the Past

Unnatural Secrets

Shadows of Solstice

The Haunting of Steely Woods

Find them all at your favorite bookseller or check us out at
MyBigFatOrangeCat.com

www.ingramcontent.com/pod-product-compliance
Lightning Source LLC
Chambersburg PA
CBHW030633190726
48286CB00008B/2502